COMPACT Research

Teenage Alcoholism

Teenage Problems

ReferencePoint Press

San Diego, CA

Other books in the Compact Research Teenage Problems set:

Teenage Drug Abuse
Teenage Eating Disorders
Teenage Mental Illness
Teenage Sex and Pregnancy
Teenage Suicide

COMPACT Research

Teenage Alcoholism

Leanne K. Currie-McGhee

Teenage Problems

ReferencePoint Press®

San Diego, CA

ReferencePoint Press®

Printed in the United States

For more information, contact:
ReferencePoint Press, Inc.
PO Box 27779
San Diego, CA 92198
www.ReferencePointPress.com

Picture credits:
Cover: iStockphoto.com and Thinkstock/Comstock
Maury Aaseng: 32–34, 46–48, 60–62, 74–76
AP Images: 15
Thinkstock/Creatas: 13

LIBRARY OF CONGRESS CATALOGING-IN-PUBLICATION DATA

Currie-McGhee, L. K. (Leanne K.)
Teenage alcoholism / by Leanne K. Currie-McGhee.
p. cm. — (Compact research series)
Includes bibliographical references and index.
ISBN-13: 978-1-60152-164-4 (hbk.)
ISBN-10: 1-60152-164-2 (hbk.)
1. Alcoholism—Juvenile literature. 2. Teenagers—Alcohol use—Juvenile literature. I. Title.
II. Series.
HV5135.C86 2012
362.2920835—dc22

2011013858

Contents

Foreword

“Where is the knowledge we have lost in information?”

—T.S. Eliot, “The Rock.”

As modern civilization continues to evolve, its ability to create, store, distribute, and access information expands exponentially. The explosion of information from all media continues to increase at a phenomenal rate. By 2020 some experts predict the worldwide information base will double every 73 days. While access to diverse sources of information and perspectives is paramount to any democratic society, information alone cannot help people gain knowledge and understanding. Information must be organized and presented clearly and succinctly in order to be understood. The challenge in the digital age becomes not the creation of information, but how best to sort, organize, enhance, and present information.

ReferencePoint Press developed the *Compact Research* series with this challenge of the information age in mind. More than any other subject area today, researching current issues can yield vast, diverse, and unqualified information that can be intimidating and overwhelming for even the most advanced and motivated researcher. The *Compact Research* series offers a compact, relevant, intelligent, and conveniently organized collection of information covering a variety of current topics ranging from illegal immigration and deforestation to diseases such as anorexia and meningitis.

The series focuses on three types of information: objective single-author narratives, opinion-based primary source quotations, and facts and statistics. The clearly written objective narratives provide context and reliable background information. Primary source quotes are carefully selected and cited, exposing the reader to differing points of view. And facts and statistics sections aid the reader in evaluating perspectives. Presenting these key types of information creates a richer, more balanced learning experience.

For better understanding and convenience, the series enhances information by organizing it into narrower topics and adding design features that make it easy for a reader to identify desired content. For example, in *Compact Research: Illegal Immigration*, a chapter covering the economic impact of illegal immigration has an objective narrative explaining the various ways the economy is impacted, a balanced section of numerous primary source quotes on the topic, followed by facts and full-color illustrations to encourage evaluation of contrasting perspectives.

The ancient Roman philosopher Lucius Annaeus Seneca wrote, "It is quality rather than quantity that matters." More than just a collection of content, the *Compact Research* series is simply committed to creating, finding, organizing, and presenting the most relevant and appropriate amount of information on a current topic in a user-friendly style that invites, intrigues, and fosters understanding.

Teenage Alcoholism at a Glance

Alcohol Dependence

Teens throughout the United States drink on a regular basis, and as a result, many become addicted. The *2009 National Survey on Drug Use and Health* found that approximately 1.2 million youth in the United States were dependent on alcohol.

Genetic Influences

Some teenagers are more prone to alcoholism than others, with children of alcoholic parents being four times as likely as their peers to develop drinking problems.

Risk Factors at Home and at School

The risk of alcoholism is higher among teenagers who live around frequent alcohol and drug abuse or who attend schools where such behaviors are common.

Physical Dangers

Alcoholism in teenagers can have lasting effects that may include damage to the developing brain, which may affect memory and concentration, and liver damage, which can be fatal.

Drinking and Driving

Drinking is a major cause of teen driving fatalities. The National Highway Traffic Safety Administration reports that 23 percent of teenage drivers involved in fatal car crashes had blood-alcohol levels over the legal limit.

Risky Behavior

When teenagers drink alcohol they are more likely to engage in risky behavior such as unprotected sex, driving while drunk, and getting into fights.

Alcohol-Caffeine Drinks

A dangerous new binge-drinking trend among young drinkers is the mixing of alcohol with super-caffeinated energy drinks. While straight alcohol might cause a person to get sleepy or even pass out, these mixed drinks keep people awake and often they continue drinking much more than they would normally consume.

Treatment

Several different types of treatment are available for alcoholics; however, only a small percentage of these programs are designed specifically for teens, and those that do exist are usually very expensive.

Prevention

The best way for teenagers to decrease their risk of developing alcoholism is to delay experimenting with alcohol. Studies show that the older teens are before they first drink alcohol, the lower their risk of becoming dependent on it.

Overview

"When you have alcoholism, you lose control over your drinking. You may not be able to control when you drink, how much you drink, or how long you drink on each occasion."

—Mayo Clinic, an internationally renowned medical practice and medical research organization.

"Alcohol is the most commonly used and abused drug among youth in the United States, more than tobacco and illicit drugs."

—Centers for Disease Control and Prevention, a US federal health agency.

What Is Alcoholism?

Alcoholism is a disorder described as an uncontrollable need for alcohol. An alcoholic's need for alcohol overrides all other needs in the person's life. This need negatively impacts most areas of an alcoholic's life—from health to relationships. For teenagers, dependence on alcohol can result in physical problems, bad grades, jail or juvenile detention, and broken relationships with friends and family.

Alcoholism can ruin a teenager's life, but with support and treatment many teen alcoholics are able to stop drinking and rebuild their lives. Treatment programs and counseling can help teens learn how to handle stressful situations without turning to alcohol and to lead productive and fulfilling lives. However, they will always have to work at staying sober and deal with their alcoholism for the rest of their lives.

How Serious Is Teenage Alcoholism?

Over 1 million teenagers in the United States suffer from alcoholism. According to the *National Survey on Drug Use and Health*, in 2009 an estimated 15.4 million people in the United States abused alcohol. Of these, 1.2 million (4.8 percent of the youth population in the United States) were young people aged 12 to 17.

A major problem associated with teenage alcoholism is that very few teenage alcoholics actually get the treatment that they need. In 2009 approximately 10 percent, or 96,000, of the teenagers classified as dependent on alcohol actually received treatment at a specialty facility such as a hospital, inpatient or outpatient rehabilitation facility, or mental health center. Those who do not get treatment run the risk of alcoholism significantly impacting the rest of their lives. The sooner teenage alcoholics start treatment, the greater the chance of recovering and rebuilding their lives.

> **“Very few teenage alcoholics actually get the treatment that they need.”**

Laura is a recovered alcoholic. She suffered the consequences of alcoholism as a teenager before attending a treatment center and taking part in Alcoholics Anonymous (AA). She allowed AA, the organization that revolves around meetings of alcoholics who are working to stay sober, to publish her story as a way to encourage other teens to get sober. Laura began drinking heavily at age 13. Soon her drinking increased to the point that she ended up in a hospital for alcohol poisoning. Following that, she dropped out of high school, ran away from home, and got arrested for stealing to fund her drinking. A judge sent her to a rehabilitation boarding school where she got treatment for substance abuse. This, according to Laura, saved her life. She continued to attend AA meetings after she left boarding school. “Today I am 19 years old, still sober, and attending college,” says Laura. “I have my family back; I have dignity; I have serenity.”[1]

Younger Drinkers

Teenagers throughout the United States attend parties and drink alcohol casually. Many are not concerned or aware that drinking increases their chances of becoming dependent on alcohol. According to the National Institute on Alcohol Abuse and Alcoholism (NIAAA), a person who begins drinking as a young teen is four times more likely to develop alcohol dependence than someone who waits until adulthood to try alcohol. The 2009 *National Survey on Drug Use and Health* found that 16.5 percent of adults who first drank at age 14 or younger, 9.4 percent of those who first tried at age 15 to 17, and 4.4 percent who first used alcohol at age 18 to 20 went on to become dependent on alcohol compared with just 2.5 percent of adults who first tried alcohol at age 21 or older.

"Having friends who drink raises the likelihood that a teen will drink."

Gwen, who is recovering from alcoholism after joining AA, was just 11 years old when she first tried alcohol. She liked the way it made her relax, and she began to drink with friends on a regular basis. Soon hangovers and blackouts were a regular part of her life. When she turned 15, she did not even know it was her own birthday until she happened to look at a newspaper and see the date. A few weeks after she turned 15, Gwen was involved in a car accident. Her friend was driving; Gwen was so drunk at the time, she remembers little more than waking up in the hospital with two broken legs. At this point she realized that she needed help. She began attending AA meetings, where she learned how to deal with life's problems without turning to drinking. For four years she has remained sober. Her story appears on the AA website. "I go to a lot of A.A. meetings and being sober is the most important thing in my life," she says. "If I'm not sober, I don't have anything—friends, a place to live, a high school diploma, or anything to hope for. Sober now, I haven't forgotten my own birthday in four years."[2]

Peer Pressure

Teenagers begin drinking for many reasons, with one of the most common being peer pressure. Having friends who drink raises the likelihood that a teen will drink. This is one of the findings in the 2010 *National Survey of American Attitudes on Substance Abuse XV: Teens and Parents.* The survey found that teens who have friends who drink regularly are

Alcohol is the most commonly used and abused drug among youth in the United States. Those who begin drinking at an early age run the greatest risk of becoming alcoholics.

almost six times more likely to drink than peers who say that none of their friends drink regularly.

Having friends who drink influenced one 15-year-old alcoholic whose story appears on the ReachOut website of Inspire USA Foundation, a nonprofit organization that works to promote mental health among youth. She explains that she started drinking while hanging out with a guy who drank. She stopped drinking after they stopped seeing each other, but then they started spending time together again. "I fell back into drinking my junior year," she writes. "I was hanging out with the same guy again and he was still drinking, so I started again."[3] Finally, she realized how drinking was affecting her life, and she stopped the relationship. Since then she has been able to stay away from drinking by no longer hanging out with others who drink.

School environment can also increase (or decrease) the risk of teen drinking. Teenagers who attend schools where drugs and alcohol are prevalent are more likely to drink alcohol. Specifically, teens who attend schools where drugs are present on campus are three times more likely to use alcohol than teens who attend schools that are drug and alcohol free.

How Alcohol Affects Teens

Alcohol is a depressant that affects every part of the human body. After a person drinks, the alcohol is carried through the bloodstream to the brain, stomach, internal organs, liver, kidneys, and muscles. It is absorbed very quickly (within 5–10 minutes) and can stay in the body for several hours.

Once it is absorbed, alcohol affects the central nervous system, causing drinkers to loosen up, relax, and feel more comfortable. This relaxation also lowers the drinker's inhibitions; in some people this can lead to embarrassing or dangerous behavior. In some drinkers, the effect on the central nervous system leads to more aggressive behavior.

> **"Alcohol abuse can negatively affect the development of the teenage brain."**

Teenagers may feel more intense effects from alcohol than adults do because their bodies are still developing and because they are unused to alcohol. With teenagers, lowered inhibitions lead to risky behavior including unprotected sex, trying illegal drugs, getting into fights, and driving while intoxicated.

What Are the Dangers of Teenage Alcoholism?

Every year thousands of teenagers are hospitalized due to alcohol-related accidents, with some of these accidents resulting in death. The most common cause of these injuries and deaths is drunk driving, but other accidents, such as falling from a window at a college party due to being inebriated, also result in deaths and injuries. In 2008, according to the Centers for Disease Control and Prevention (CDC), there were approximately 190,000 emergency room visits by persons under age 21 for injuries and other conditions linked to alcohol.

Most of the alcohol-related injuries seen by hospitals were caused

High school students weep during a true-to-life presentation about underage drinking and driving. Nearly a quarter of teenage drivers involved in fatal car crashes have blood-alcohol levels over the legal limit.

by drunk driving, another dangerous consequence of teenage drinking. In November 2010 driving while drunk ended the life of 18-year-old Matthew Alston of the United Kingdom. Friends and family remember Alston as a popular young man with a lot of academic potential and athletic talent. On that day, Alston had come home from a party at 5:30 a.m. but could not sleep and decided to go for a drive around 7:00 a.m. Other drivers saw his car speeding along a road before he lost control and smashed into another vehicle traveling in the opposite direction. Police reported that he had been driving under the influence of alcohol.

Brain Development Impaired

Alcohol abuse can negatively affect the development of the teenage brain. This is because during adolescence both the prefrontal cortex and hippocampus in the brain are still developing. Chronic alcohol use and binge drinking, when teens drink five drinks or more at one setting, hinder the prefrontal cortex and hippocampus from developing properly. This damage can be long-term and irreversible.

Decision making, judgment, learning ability, and memory are most affected. The prefrontal cortex of the brain is the area that is responsible for thinking, planning, and good judgment. The hippocampus is involved with learning and memory. Studies by the American Medical Association (AMA), for instance, found that youth aged 14 to 21 who had abused alcohol had a 10 percent smaller hippocampus than youth who were nondrinkers. This damage can permanently impair a teenager's memory and learning ability.

"Diagnosing alcoholism is one of the more difficult aspects of getting treatment for a teenage alcoholic."

Neuroscientist Susan Tapert conducted studies of the effects of drinking on teens' learning abilities and found negative consequences in both males and females. "For girls who had been engaging in heavy drinking during adolescence, it looks like they're performing more poorly on tests of spatial functioning, which links to mathematics, engineering kinds of functions," says Tapert. "For boys who engaged in binge drinking during adolescence, we see poor performance on tests of attention—[that is,] being able to focus on something that might be somewhat boring, for a sustained period of time."[4]

Pediatrician Alcohol Screening

Diagnosing alcoholism is one of the more difficult aspects of getting treatment for a teenage alcoholic. According to the Substance Abuse and Mental Health Services Administration (SAMHSA), most adolescents with substance abuse problems are unlikely to recognize their need for treatment. Often people, including a teen's own parents and teachers, believe the teenager is just behaving badly as opposed to demonstrating signs of alcohol dependence. If a teen's alcoholism goes untreated, getting sober will become more difficult for him or her as time passes. To combat this problem, health care professionals and organizations that have routine contact with adolescents are using procedures to identify abuse problems and refer adolescents to care.

In 2010 the AMA's *Guidelines for Adolescent Preventive Services* and the American Academy of Pediatrics' *Bright Futures* guidelines recommended that pediatricians and other health care providers who work with children and adolescents conduct routine annual substance abuse screening of their patients. One issue with such screening, however, is that some parents believe they should be in the room with the doctor while their teen is asked questions. Health professionals claim this can be a barrier to getting honest answers from teens. "We want to keep families involved," Patricia Kokotailo, director of adolescent medicine at the University of Wisconsin School of Medicine and Public Health said, "but some things are very difficult for teenagers to express if it's not confidential."[5]

How Is Teenage Alcoholism Treated?

Most alcohol treatment programs, whether for adults or teenagers, attempt to do more than simply reduce or stop the use of alcohol. The major focus is to get alcoholics to change their lifestyles and to develop skills for dealing with life's difficulties so that they no longer feel the need for alcohol. In addition to accomplishing this, treatment programs for teens need to take into consideration teenagers' family situations, peer pressure, and education. A variety of different treatment programs are available for teenage alcoholics, including residential and outpatient treatment centers, self-help groups such as AA, individual and group counseling, and family counseling.

> **Treatment programs for teens need to take into consideration teenagers' family situations, peer pressure, and education.**

The most common type of program for teenagers is the outpatient substance abuse treatment center, which allows teens to live at home and attend school while undergoing treatment. According to SAMHSA's *National Survey of Substance Abuse Treatment Services*, 88 percent of adolescents who received substance abuse treatment in 2008 did so in outpatient treatment centers. Because the teens continue to live at home, family members can take part in family counseling. This is important because creating open communication and stable relationships between teens and their parents is an integral part of the recovery process.

Some teenage alcoholics seek help at inpatient substance abuse treatment centers. Eleven percent of adolescents who received substance abuse treatment in 2008 were enrolled in an inpatient treatment center. Inpatient treatment is most often used for teens who have previously completed outpatient treatment then relapsed. Relapses are a common occurrence among recovering alcoholics of all ages. Inpatient facilities provide 24-hour oversight and care for especially vulnerable teenagers.

Interventions

Denial is a characteristic of alcoholism, whether the alcoholic is an adult or a teenager. When teen alcoholics fail to recognize or acknowledge that they have a problem, family and friends may plan an intervention to correct this.

During an intervention, the teen alcoholic is brought to a place where family and/or friends are gathered. Usually an experienced facilitator guides the meeting. The facilitator will ask all participants to talk about their love for the teen with the alcohol problem as well as how his or her alcoholism is negatively affecting all of their lives. After listening to the speakers, it is up to the alcoholic to decide whether or not to seek treatment. "Though few teens will initially embrace the idea of teen alcohol rehab, the goal is that they will fully understand the need for treatment by the end of the intervention,"[6] states the Newport Academy, a substance abuse treatment center for adolescents. At interventions the goal is to get teenagers to understand how their alcohol use has hurt others and then decide for themselves that they need treatment.

Unlike adults, however, teenagers have only so much say on the question of treatment. Because most teenagers are minors, parents can force an alcoholic teen to take part in a treatment program. In most cases this sort of option would involve a highly structured inpatient facility.

Detoxification

All alcoholism treatment begins with detoxification, which is the process in which the body rids itself of alcohol and adjusts to functioning without it. Depending on how long the individual has been habitually using alcohol, this can be a very difficult process. People react differently, both mentally and physcially, as their bodies adjust to the lack of alcohol in their systems.

When a teen undergoes alcohol detoxification, he or she will likely experience a series of withdrawal symptoms. While the severity of symptoms varies depending on the intensity and depth of the addiction, most alcoholics experience the same basic reactions. Common reactions include shakiness or seizures, irritability, anxiety, depression, mood swings, cravings for alcohol, and (in extreme cases) hallucinations. These symptoms can be so severe that some alcoholics will start drinking again to alleviate the symptoms. However, alcoholics who complete the detoxification process can then concentrate on ways to remain sober and learn how to deal with life without alcohol.

Can Teenage Alcoholism Be Prevented?

The best way to prevent teenagers from becoming alcoholics is to keep them from experimenting with drinking. One of the ways to do this is to identify teenagers who are at risk of drinking and teach them how to cope with their situations without alcohol. Many teens at high risk for alcohol abuse are those going through major transitions in their lives.

The divorce of parents, for example, usually causes a major transition in a teen's life. According to SAMHSA, most children of divorced parents in the United States (40 percent of all children) adjust well to their parents' divorce, but 20 to 25 percent of these children have major trouble dealing with this change. Some teens deal with the divorce by turning to alcohol. Divorce counseling is one way to help prevent this. Studies have found that teens who attend divorce counseling have a reduced risk of making alcohol and drugs part of their coping mechanism.

> **"Some teens deal with divorce by turning to alcohol."**

Divorce is not the only life change that can result in teenagers' drinking. Several other changes can result in stress that drives them to drink. "During periods of transition, certain life events—such as going from middle school to high school, moving to a different neighborhood, the effect of divorce, separation or death, the birth of additional children, breaking up with a significant other—can cause children to turn to alcohol as a solution,"[7] states the Everything Addiction website, a website dedicated to providing information about addiction. For this reason, teenage alcohol prevention programs exist in schools and communities throughout the nation. The main goal of these programs is to teach teenagers constructive ways to deal with their life issues so they do not turn to drinking.

Even with the many prevention programs throughout the United States, over 1 million teenagers are dependent on alcohol. Due to the severe consequences of teenage alcoholism, it is a major health issue. Recent studies show that teenage drinking has remained steady in recent years, so teenage alcoholism is likely to remain a problem that must be dealt with.

How Serious Is Teenage Alcoholism?

> "Alcohol, the most widely used and abused drug among youth, causes serious and potentially life-threatening problems for teens."

—Steve Frisch, a clinical psychologist in Chicago, Illinois.

> "By a wide margin, teenagers abuse alcohol more than any other substance. It is legal and widely available. Nationwide, teens with alcohol dependency are the majority of adolescents admitted for treatment."

—Supporting materials for *The Addiction Project*, produced by HBO in partnership with the Robert Wood Johnson Foundation, the National Institute on Drug Abuse, and the National Institute on Alcohol Abuse and Alcoholism.

Alcohol is the drug most commonly used by teenagers. According to the CDC, people aged 12 to 20 drink 11 percent of all alcohol consumed in the United States. Additionally, the rate of current alcohol use among youths aged 12 to 17 was 14.7 percent in 2009. This rate helps explain the finding that over 1 million youths in the United States have alcohol problems.

One of the dangerous aspects of teenage drinking is that the younger a person is when he or she first drinks, the greater the person's risk of developing alcoholism. The National Institute on Alcohol Abuse and Alcoholism (NIAAA) reports that teenagers who begin drinking before age 15 are four times more likely to become alcoholics than those who do not drink until they are older.

Easy Access

Teenage alcoholism usually starts with social drinking—that is, small or large groups of kids drinking at parties or informal gatherings. Although it is illegal for teens to drink alcohol, it is relatively easy for them to get it. In the 2010 *National Survey of American Attitudes on Substance Abuse XV: Teens and Parents* survey, teenagers were asked what substance is easiest to get, and 26 percent answered beer; only cigarettes, a legal substance for those aged 18 and over, was higher, at 27 percent. Additionally, 27 percent of those surveyed said that they could get alcohol in less than an hour if they wanted to do so.

Throughout the nation, local surveys confirm that it is not difficult for teenagers to get alcohol. In 2010 a newspaper survey in Roanoke, Virginia, found that 45 percent of middle school students and more than 80 percent of high school students surveyed in the Roanoke area said alcohol is "very easy" to obtain. One of the reasons alcohol is so easy to obtain is that teenagers often know someone—an older friend or sibling—who will legally buy the alcohol and give it to the teens. For the most part, if a teenager is interested in drinking alcohol, he or she will be able to find a way to get it.

When Use Becomes Alcoholism

There is a difference between use, abuse, and addiction. Drinking alcohol occasionally and not excessively is considered use, not abuse. Abuse is drinking alcohol when it negatively affects other areas of the drinker's life. Teenagers who skip school on a regular basis because they are hungover from partying are considered to have an abuse problem. Addiction, or alcoholism, is the inabilty to get through the day without feeling the uncontrollable urge to drink and experiencing withdrawal symptoms when not drinking. People addicted to alcohol are classified as alcoholics.

Kevin is a recovering alcoholic. He described the descent into teen alcoholism to substance abuse counselors at Boonshoft School of Medicine at Wright State University in Ohio. When Kevin started drinking in high school, he was just a casual drinker but it was not long before his drinking escalated. On the day he graduated from high school, Kevin recalls, he and a few friends stole alcohol from a convenience store and drank until they passed out. Months after that, he was involved in a car accident that resulted in the deaths of three people. Kevin remembers driving with a friend to his second job and deciding not to go to work. Instead he and his friend went drinking. He does not recall exactly what happened, but he ended up driving and causing an accident. "The next thing I remember was being in the hospital in a halo with a broken neck with my jaws wired and a staff person telling me a severe car accident had almost taken my life."[8] He was found guilty of reckless homicide and sentenced to spend time in prison.

> **If a teenager is interested in drinking alcohol, he or she will be able to find a way to get it.**

Years later, when his wife left him and he got arrested for buying drugs, Kevin finally recognized he needed help. He became sober after attending a court-ordered treatment program and has remained sober while attending Alcoholics Anonymous (AA) meetings.

Symptoms of Alcoholism

A person who no longer has control of his or her life because of drinking may exhibit symptoms of alcoholism. For example, teenage alcoholics will often miss school, drive drunk, get in trouble with the law, and fight with parents as a result of their drinking. Other common symptoms of alcoholism among teenagers include lying, breaking curfew, becoming verbally or physically abusive toward others, experiencing mood swings, stealing, and making changes in friends.

Withdrawal symptoms are another sign of alcoholism in someone who tries to stop drinking. These symptoms occur because the alcoholic's body has become accustomed to functioning with the help of alcohol. The withdrawal usually occurs within 5–10 hours after the last drink. Minor symptoms include shakiness, anxiety, and fatigue; more severe symptoms include tremors, nausea, and insomnia. The more a person has been drinking, the more likely that person will develop alcohol withdrawal symptoms when he or she stops. According to Bill Urell, an addiction therapist, "Alcohol withdrawal symptoms generally occur with habitual drinkers. The reason for this is their body has become . . . used to high levels of alcohol intake, and actually goes through a shock when the intake is suddenly stopped."[9]

Why Do Teenagers Use Alcohol?

No one starts drinking with the intent of becoming an alcoholic—and teens are no exception. The reasons they start drinking are varied. Most teenagers start drinking for social reasons: If alcohol flows freely at a party or if their friends are drinking, it may be hard for a teen to resist joining in. Teens will drink to feel part of the group and continue drinking if it encourages acceptance by their peers.

Cathy wanted to feel at ease around other teenagers and had trouble doing that on her own. She began drinking at age 14 while attending summer camp, she told substance abuse counselors at Boonshoft School of Medicine. She did this because she saw it as a way to gain acceptance from other kids at the camp. Cathy had been born with muscular dystrophy, a disease that causes muscle tissue to become weak over time and can result in loss of motor skills and difficulties walking. For Cathy, muscular dystrophy meant that she had to use a wheelchair, which made her feel different from other kids. And then, during her teenage years, she also realized that she was a lesbian, adding to her feelings of being an outsider. She thought that drinking would help her to be more sociable around other people. "Drinking alcohol would help me to feel more at ease in these settings,"[10] she says.

> **"Teenage alcoholics will often miss school, drive drunk, get in trouble with the law, and fight with parents as a result of their drinking."**

By the time she was in her twenties Cathy was drinking so much that she would pass out on a regular basis. It was then she realized that she was an alcoholic. Cathy was invited by a friend to attend an AA meeting and agreed to go. The meetings had a positive effect on her, and she realized she needed to change her life. She became sober after receiving treatment at the Boonshoft School of Medicine and has remained so since that time.

Dealing with Family Issues

Teenagers who live in unstable or troubled settings are more likely to drink and become addicted to alcohol than are other teens. The National Institute on Drug Abuse (NIDA) has reported that living in a home where a close family member has an alcohol or drug problem can heighten the alcoholism risk for teens. Sometimes teens turn to alcohol to escape violence or arguments that might occur in a home with an alcoholic or drug abuser. This is not a guarantee of future alcohol problems, however; life with an alcoholic sometimes has the opposite effect of instilling determination in that teen to never use such substances.

> **Living in a home where a close family member has an alcohol or drug problem can heighten the alcoholism risk for teens.**

Another risk factor for teenagers getting involved with alcohol is having a weak relationship with their parents. According to the 2010 *National Survey of American Attitudes on Substance Abuse XV: Teens and Parents*, teens in families with weak family ties are almost three times more likely to have tried alcohol than are teens in families with strong family ties. Having weak family ties, however, does not necessarily mean that a teenager will drink. Teens without close relationships to their parents may deal with this by becoming self-sufficient and strong rather than turning to drugs and alcohol.

Genetics Play a Role

One of the biggest risk factors for alcoholism is being biologically related to someone who is an alcoholic. Current evidence indicates that in both men and women, alcoholism is 50 to 60 percent genetically determined. Specifically, scientists have discovered a collection of genes that certain people carry that increases an individual's risk of developing addiction problems. A person with this collection of genes would be more likely to become addicted to alcohol if he or she begins to drink socially, while someone without these genes would be less likely to become addicted. Having a biological parent who is an alcoholic does not mean the child is certain to develop alcoholism; however, it does mean the child has a greater risk than others of becoming an alcoholic.

> **"Having a biological parent who is an alcoholic does not mean the child is certain to develop alcoholism."**

If teens have knowledge of their higher risk they can prevent alcoholism by not drinking. Roxie Norman grew up with an alcoholic father, and dealing with his alcoholism kept her from engaging in social drinking as a teenager. "I personally feel that it was my father's alcoholism that made me decide early on in my own life to not fall into the trap of becoming addicted to alcohol," writes Roxie. "The life that I lived as a young child that was always around an alcoholic . . . was this very thing that helped me to learn the negative things that alcohol can bring to those that may become addicted and for that I'm thankful because I will never drink alcohol."[11]

Multiple Addictions

Many alcoholics are not just addicted to alcohol. Many are also addicted to other substances, such as cigarettes. Statistics show that between 70 and 80 percent of alcoholics smoke cigarettes. The NIAAA reports that people who are dependent on alcohol are three times more likely then those in the general population to be smokers.

Combining alcohol and illegal substances is also not uncommon among addicts. A teenage alcoholic might use a stimulant drug such as methamphetamine to get energy during the day and then use alcohol to settle down at night. The 2009 *National Survey on Drug Use and Health* found that 3.2 million people in the United States were considered dependent on or abusing both alcohol and illicit drugs. According to the same survey, 69.9 percent of heavy-drinking youths aged 12 to 17 were also using illicit drugs.

Being addicted to one substance is dangerous enough, being addicted to more than one increases a teen's chances of getting into an accident, dropping out of school, getting into fights, and developing health problems. Sarah T. experienced many of these problems as a teenager due to her alcohol and cocaine addiction. She grew up without a father and often fought with her mother. To escape her problems she turned to alcohol. "I went on a church trip once and there I tasted alcohol for the first time. I loved it. Something just clicked inside of me. I no longer felt the bad feelings I once did,"[12] Sarah writes. Her story appears on the website About.com. Before long she was also smoking marijuana, popping pills, and snorting cocaine. Sarah's mother placed her in a treatment center but she relapsed. However, she soon realized she was ruining her life and began to attend AA. By the time she was 18 years old, Sarah was sober and getting ready to attend college.

Teens who have multiple addictions to alcohol and drugs or a single addiction to alcohol are putting themselves in serious danger with their substance abuse. Teenage alcoholism is negatively affecting teens around the country. These teens may end up with serious physical, emotional, and social problems if they do not get help for their addiction.

Primary Source Quotes*

How Serious Is Teenage Alcoholism?

"The teen years are a time where peer acceptance is a deep need among teens. There is a strong desire to fit in to one's social group and this can lead to alcohol and other drug initiation."

—Jeff Wolfsberg, Q&A interview, "An Interview with Jeff Wolfsberg," About.com, 2009. http://privateschool.about.com.

Wolfsberg is an internationally recognized expert in drug education, a radio talk show host, and a writer.

"To take one drink is to awaken the sleeping beast."

—Melissa Gilbert, Q&A interview, "Think Your Kids or Grandkids Are Abusing Drugs or Alcohol?," ThirdAge.com, January 6, 2011. www.thirdage.com.

Gilbert, an actress, recovering alcoholic, and spokesperson for Partnership at Drugfree.org, discusses what it is like to be addicted to alcohol.

* Editor's Note: While the definition of a primary source can be narrowly or broadly defined, for the purposes of Compact Research, a primary source consists of: 1) results of original research presented by an organization or researcher; 2) eyewitness accounts of events, personal experience, or work experience; 3) first-person editorials offering pundits' opinions; 4) government officials presenting political plans and/or policies; 5) representatives of organizations presenting testimony or policy.

"Unfortunately, far too many parents treat underage drinking as no big deal; often with an 'at least he's not doing drugs' mentality. Alcohol is a mind-altering drug as evidenced by the alcohol manufacturer's advertisement, 'Friends don't let friends drive drunk.'"

—Jim May, "Mom Worries About College-Age Son's Drinking Habits," mywesttexas.com, January 23, 2011. www.mywesttexas.com.

May is a family therapist who writes a column for the *Midland (TX) Reporter-Telegram.*

"Most alcoholics not only don't know they are alcoholics in the early years of their drinking, but they look around and see others who drink too much and think that they are glad that they are not like this one or that one. The ability to lie to oneself is limitless."

—Monte Canfield, "I Am an Alcoholic, Part Two," *Salon,* July 12, 2010. http://open.salon.com.

Canfield is a retired minister and a recovering alcoholic who writes a blog about his battle with alcoholism.

"Peer pressure is the number one reason that teens drink alcohol. The need for social acceptance among peer groups is tremendous and kids will engage in many behaviors in which parents may not approve in order to be accepted by a social group."

—Susan McConnell, "Parental Influence in Underage Drinking," October 19, 2009. http://susanbmcconnell.com.

McConnell is a motivational speaker and author who focuses on parenting.

"Remember: Risk is not destiny. Just because alcoholism tends to run in families doesn't mean that a child of an alcoholic parent will automatically become an alcoholic too."

—FACE, "Questions About Alcoholism," 2010. www.faceproject.org.

The FACE Project is a nonprofit organization with the mission to promote positive social and character development among school children.

"There's no question that drinking is a problem in most high schools. Alcohol is our most pervasive drug. Teens have access to it at parties, can obtain it from older friends who are of legal age to buy it, or may simply raid their parents' liquor cabinets."

—American Academy of Child & Adolescent Psychiatry, "Teens: Alcohol and Other Drugs," May 2008. http://aacap.org.

The American Academy of Child & Adolescent Psychiatry is the leading national association of professionals in that field of medicine.

"Many adults still believe that drinking is a rite of passage and a normal part of growing up. They believe that youth are just experimenting. . . . Some adult attitudes and inaction have been identified as contributing to the fact that alcohol causes youth more harm than all illegal drugs, combined."

—Cathy Wendholt-McDade, "Wake Up to Teen Binge Drinking," *Atlanta Journal-Constitution*, November 24, 2010.

Wendholt-McDade is board vice chair of the Cobb Alcohol Taskforce, an organization that works to reduce underage drinking and youth binge drinking.

Facts and Illustrations

How Serious Is Teenage Alcoholism?

- According to the 2009 Monitoring the Future survey, nearly **three-quarters** of students (72 percent) have consumed alcohol by the end of high school.
- The 2009 Monitoring the Future survey found that more than **37 percent** of students have consumed alcohol by the end of eighth grade.
- According to the *National Survey on Drug Use and Health*, in 2009, **7 percent** of all US youths aged 12 to 17 were classified as dependent on alcohol.
- According to the 2010 *National Survey of American Attitudes on Substance Abuse XV: Teens and Parents*, **27 percent** of youths surveyed said they could get alcohol within an hour, **10 percent** within a few hours, and **10 percent** within a day.
- The 2009 Monitoring the Future survey found that **57 percent** of twelfth graders and **17 percent** of eighth graders reported having been drunk at least once in their life.
- The 2009 CDC's Youth Risk Behavior Surveillance System found that **24.2 percent** of US teens had had 5 or more drinks of alcohol in a row on at least one day during the 30 days before the survey.
- Youth exposure to alcohol advertising on US television increased **71 percent** between 2001 and 2009, according to a 2009 analysis by the Center on Alcohol Marketing and Youth at the Johns Hopkins Bloomberg School of Public Health.

Teen Drinking Is Common

Public health officials are concerned about the number of teenagers who drink alcohol. The earlier that teens begin drinking, the higher the likelihood they will become alcoholics. This chart shows the percentage of white, Hispanic, and black high school students who drank alcohol within 30 days of a 2009 survey. In all cases, over 30 percent of the teens admitted to drinking.

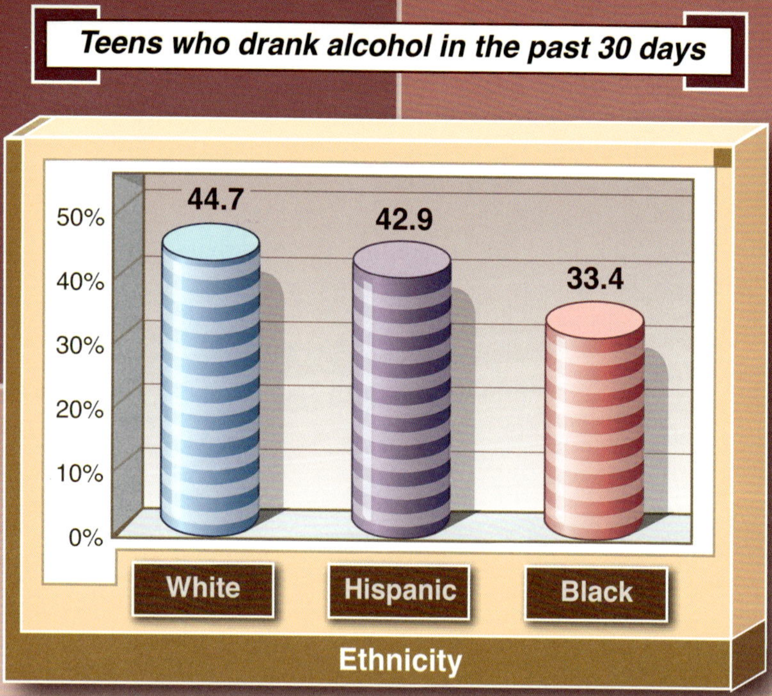

Source: Centers for Disease Control and Prevention, *Morbidity and Mortality Weekly Report*, June 4, 2010, p. 73. www.cdc.gov.

- According to the 2008 report *Impact of Alcohol Advertising and Media Exposure on Adolescent Alcohol Use: A Systematic Review of Longitudinal Studies*, exposure to alcohol **advertisements in magazines** and other media influences teen decisions on drinking.

Teen Alcohol Dependence and Abuse Decreasing

Overall, in the past decade alcohol abuse and dependence among youth has decreased. From 2002 to 2009 the percentage of youth in the United States aged 12 to 17 who were dependent on or abusing alcohol dropped from 5.9 percent to 4.6 percent.

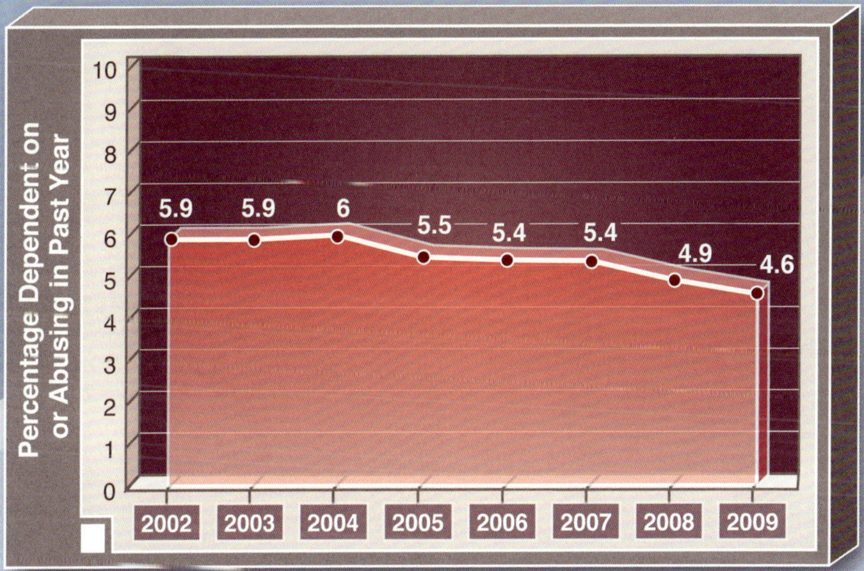

Source: US Department of Health and Human Services, *National Survey on Drug Use and Health*, 2009. www.drugabusestatistics.samhsa.gov.

- The Partnership at Drugfree.org used the 2009 *Partnership Attitude Tracking Study* to determine that the number of middle school and high school girls who say they drink had increased from 53 percent in 2008 to **59 percent** in 2009.

- The 2009 *National Survey on Drug Use and Health* reports that among heavy alcohol users aged 12 or older, **56.3 percent** also smoked cigarettes in the month before the survey.

Teen Access to Alcohol

One reason that teenage drinking is common is that teens are able to obtain alcohol easily. According to a 2010 survey by Columbia University's National Center on Addiction and Substance Abuse, 37 percent of teens say they can get alcohol within a day or less.

Question: If you wanted to get alcohol right now, how long would it take you to get it?

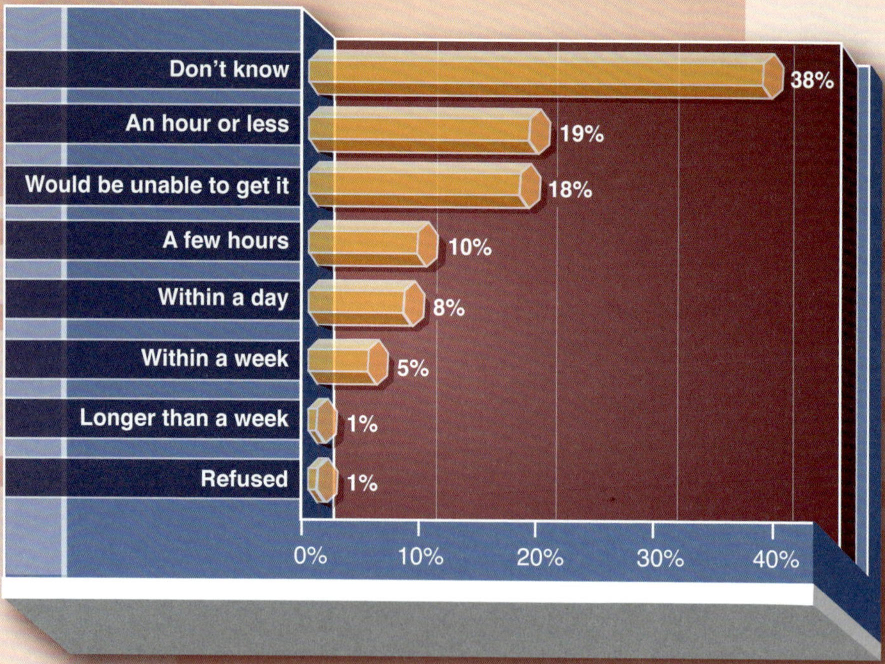

Source: Outside the Classroom, "Student Interest in Alcohol Free Events," 2008. www.outsidetheclassroom.com.

- The *2009 National Survey on Drug Use and Health* found that among youths aged 12 to 17 who were heavy drinkers, **69.9 percent** were also using illicit drugs.

What Are the Dangers of Teenage Alcoholism?

“Alcohol and street drugs cause impairment and damage to developing organs including the brain and female reproductive system. Using them can lead to automobile accidents, unprotected sex, and other hazards.”

—Aspen Education Group, provider of education programs for young people who deal with issues such as substance abuse.

“The Holiday Season was marred by another tragic death when a 17-year-old Redding student was found unconscious in the bathroom of her friend’s house. The two had been drinking after the parents had apparently gone to bed. Alcohol poisoning was determined to be the cause of death.”

—Todd Slaughter, an attorney in California who often deals with alcohol-related cases.

Most current research on teens and alcohol focuses on excessive drinking as opposed to alcoholism. But the worry, experts say, is that once excessive drinking becomes entrenched, the distance a teenager must travel to full-blown alcoholism is not that far. The dangers of excessive drinking and alcoholism are intertwined.

Alcohol, in large quantities and consumed over an extended period of time, is a toxin; it can disrupt the transmission of nerve impulses in the brain and nervous system. Chronic alcohol abuse, whether in adults or teenagers, can lead to loss of balance, impotence, numbness of the feet and hands, and even blindness. Alcoholism in the heaviest drinkers sometimes also results in inflammation of the stomach and digestive system, which disrupts proper digestion and absorption of food.

> **"US hospitals admit thousands of teenagers each year for alcohol-related problems."**

Other serious conditions common among long-term alcoholics include delirium tremens and liver damage. Delirium tremens causes a person to experience mental confusion, extreme excitability, anxiety, trembling, rapid pulse, and hallucinations. Cirrhosis of the liver, brought on by long-term heavy drinking, can lead to liver failure, liver cancer, and death.

While some of these dangers occur mainly in people who have a long history of alcoholism, health officials worry that many teenagers are setting themselves up for these types of problems. United States hospitals admit thousands of teenagers each year for alcohol-related problems. In 2009, people under age 20 made 199,429 alcohol-related emergency room visits.

Driving Under the Influence

One of the most dangerous behaviors associated with teenage alcoholism is driving under the influence. Throughout the country many teenagers who drink alcohol at parties or with friends still decide to drive even though it is both illegal and dangerous. Zero-tolerance laws in all states make it illegal for youth under age 21 to drive with any measurable amount of alcohol in their systems. Because of the frequency of their drinking, alcoholic teenagers are at an even higher risk than other teens for driving while intoxicated.

According to the CDC, motor vehicle crashes rank as the top cause of death for US teenagers. Statistics show that many of these crashes are alcohol related. The National Highway Traffic Safety Administration reports that 5,470 persons under the age of 21 died in vehicle crashes in 2009. Of these, according to the Century Council, a national nonprofit organization that fights drunk driving and underage drinking, 1,398 died as a result of an alcohol-related car crash.

Brandy Graff was 18 years old when she and a friend decided to share a case of beer at the beach. On the way home from the beach she and her friend decided to go to a party, and there they drank some more. The friends then left the party, with Graff driving. On the way home, Graff crashed into another car, killing two of the people in the car and injuring a third. Graff was sentenced to 15 years in jail and is currently incarcerated. The Johnston Coalition to Prevent Substance Abuse sponsors trips by high school students to the Rhode Island Adult Correctional Institutions, where Graff is serving her time. Graff and other convicted drunk drivers speak to these students about drinking and driving in hopes of getting them to think before they do the same thing. "You don't want to be me. . . . I'm now Brandy: drunk driver. Brandy: killer,"[13] she says.

The Dangers of Binge Drinking

Drinking large amounts of alcohol in a short period of time, known as binge drinking, has become a serious problem among both alcoholic and nonalcoholic teenagers. The CDC's *2009 Youth Risk Behavior Survey* found that 24 percent of high school students questioned said that they had engaged in binge drinking within the previous 30 days. When binge drinking, teenagers also put themselves in physical danger because drinking excessive amounts of alcohol in a short period of time can seriously harm the body.

> **"The greatest dangers of alcohol poisoning are that teenagers may pass out and then stop breathing, or they may throw up and choke to death on their own vomit."**

Alcohol is first absorbed into the body through the stomach and small intestine. Next it travels through the intestines to the liver and then on to the heart, brain, muscles, and other tissues. This process typically happens very quickly, within a few minutes. As the alcohol is absorbed it depresses nerves that control involuntary actions such as breathing and the gag reflex (which prevents choking). When alcohol is drunk in large amounts and quickly, the alcohol can actually stop these functions. This condition is known as alcohol poisoning.

The greatest dangers of alcohol poisoning are that teenagers may pass out and then stop breathing, or they may throw up and choke to death on their own vomit. Despite the dangers of binge drinking, studies show that teens do not believe that drinking excessively is risky. In 2011 the Partnership at Drugfree.org reported that nearly half of the teens questioned in its study did not think drinking five or more alcoholic beverages a day was a big risk. "You're seeing this weakness in this generation of teens' attitudes around drug and alcohol use," says Steve Pasierb, president of the Partnership at Drugfree.org. "It's not like this generation of kids thinks they're more bulletproof than others, but they really don't see any harm in that heavy drinking."[14]

Alcohol's Influence on Teen Sexual Activity

One risky behavior associated with excessive teenage alcohol use is the increased likelihood of teens' engaging in sexual activity and unprotected sex. According to a 2009 New York City Department of Health survey, teens who reported drinking any amount of alcohol in the past month were more than twice as likely as nondrinkers (27 percent versus 11 percent) to report having had multiple sex partners. Additionally, the same report found that condom use was less common (63 percent) among teens who reported using alcohol or drugs before sex than among those who were sober (72 percent). Unprotected sex can lead to pregnancy and sexually transmitted diseases such as AIDS, herpes, and gonorrhea.

The possibility of rape also increases for teens who drink excessively. The National Women's Health Information Center states that alcohol is the most common drug involved in date rape. Perpetrators of the assaults will persuade their dates to drink alcohol because being intoxicated makes it more difficult to fend off attacks, particularly if she has drunk so much that she passes out.

Today Holly is a recovering alcoholic working as a middle school teacher in the Midwest, but she experienced many dark years as a teenage alcoholic. She told her story to the author of *Delaying That First Drink: A Parents' Guide* as a way to let teenagers know the dangers of drinking. As a young teen Holly drank both when she was alone and when she went to parties. On one occasion she drank so much at a party that she passed out. When she woke up she realized she had been gang raped. Although

Holly recovered from this experience and from her alcoholism, the horror of the event remains with her.

Higher Rates of Violence

Acting on impulse is a common effect of alcohol, and for teens who drink excessively this can increase their likelihood of getting involved in fights or other forms of violence. Alcohol changes a drinker's brain chemistry by altering levels of neurotransmitters, which are chemical messengers that control thought processes, behavior, and emotion. Alcohol increases the effects of the neurotransmitter that decreases inhibition. A person who is drinking is more likely to say what he or she thinks without considering the consequences, and a person who is drunk is more likely to act upon impulses, such as anger, without considering the results.

In 2008, researchers at the Liverpool John Moores University in the United Kingdom reported that 40 percent of teen girls and 42 percent of teen boys who drank at least once a week were later involved in violence. "Kids who drink are also likely to fight, whether they actually drink at the time of the fight, and are likely to be involved in other problematic behaviors,"[15] explains Maureen Walton, author on a study of teen violence and alcohol.

> **Police officers in the United States often encounter violence among underage drinkers—especially at parties.**

Police officers in the United States often encounter violence among underage drinkers—especially at parties. During one night in April 2010, police in Las Vegas handled six calls regarding incidents such as fighting and other complaints related to underage drinking at house parties—and this was considered a slow night. Las Vegas police were cracking down on underage drinking parties because earlier that year two 17-year-old girls were shot and killed at house parties. "[This crackdown] is about preventing these get-togethers and these fights. If we let [these parties continue], and these kids get progressively drunker, then you get the rub, the fight, and then we got problems,"[16] explains Lieutenant Ted Snodgrass, who has been with the Las Vegas police for 27 years.

School Problems

Academic problems such as low grades, absenteeism, and high dropout rates are common among teenagers who abuse alcohol. Studies have shown that the more a student uses alcohol, tobacco, and other drugs, the lower his or her grade point average is likely to be. The 2009 CDC's *Youth Risk Behavior Survey* discovered that the students who got bad grades drank more than those who received good grades. Sixty-eight percent of the students who received high grades reported that they did not drink alcohol, while 62 percent of students who mainly got Ds and Fs, reported they did drink alcohol.

> **“Alcohol abuse results in students missing classes due to hangovers and drinking instead of studying.”**

Dropping out of school can also result from excessive drinking. Alcohol abuse results in students missing classes due to hangovers and drinking instead of studying. The CORE Institute, the largest national alcohol and drug database on drinking and drug use by college students in the United States, found that 28 percent of all college dropouts leave school because of alcohol or other drug use.

Suicide and Teenage Drinking

Suicide is the third leading cause of death among teens and young adults 15 to 24 years of age. Alcohol abuse increases the risk of teen suicide. Georgia State University professor Monica Swahn conducted research into the link between drinking and suicide and published her work in a 2008 issue of *Pediatrics*. Swahn's findings show that those who begin drinking at a young age are three times more likely than nondrinking peers to attempt suicide.

Teenagers who turn to alcohol for help in dealing with emotional pain often find that their problems multiply, particularly if drinking escalates to alcoholism. At this point some teenagers feel that suicide is the only way to stop the pain. Julee, a recovering alcoholic, told her story in an Alcoholics Anonymous (AA) brochure to help other teens dealing with alcoholism. At age 14 Julee longed to be beautiful, popular, and an excellent athlete, but instead she felt ugly and unpopular. She began drinking regularly because when she drank she felt more confident. She often drank at parties because of the confidence it gave her but soon found herself needing to drink more and more to feel this confidence. Eventually she was drinking so much that she often blacked out. During these blackouts, she was sexually assaulted more than once and often woke up in strange places, scared and alone.

Julee felt so hopeless that she attempted suicide. Her parents committed her to a treatment center for substance abuse and mental health help. She relapsed twice; after the second relapse Julee finally realized that she was an alcoholic and wanted to live. "I realized I did not want to die anymore," she says, "that I did not want to drink anymore."[17] Julee has remained sober for more than 15 years. The consequences of alcoholism can ruin a teenager's future, but being an alcoholic, as Julee found, does not make that a certainty. Treatment can change a teenage alcoholic's life, putting alcoholism's consequences in the past.

Primary Source Quotes*

What Are the Dangers of Teenage Alcoholism?

"Drinking is a problem if it causes trouble in your relationships, in school, in social activities, or in how you think and feel."

—Centers for Disease Control and Prevention, "Alcohol and Public Health," July 20, 2010. http://www.cdc.gov.

The Centers for Disease Control and Prevention is a US government agency dedicated to protecting health and promoting quality of life through the prevention and control of disease, injury, and disability.

"Although alcohol consumption by adolescents is often regarded as a rite of passage, it is a serious threat to adolescent development and health."

—Office of the Surgeon General, *Surgeon General's Perspectives*, vol. 124, January/February 2009. www.surgeongeneral.gov.

The Office of the Surgeon General oversees the Commissioned Corps of the US Public Health Service and is a part of the US Department of Health and Human Services.

---

* Editor's Note: While the definition of a primary source can be narrowly or broadly defined, for the purposes of Compact Research, a primary source consists of: 1) results of original research presented by an organization or researcher; 2) eyewitness accounts of events, personal experience, or work experience; 3) first-person editorials offering pundits' opinions; 4) government officials presenting political plans and/or policies; 5) representatives of organizations presenting testimony or policy.

“When the brain is most vulnerable is also the time when teens are most likely to experiment with drugs or alcohol. Sometimes when I'm working with teens, I . . . try to reason with them that if they're doing drugs or alcohol that evening, it may not just be affecting their brains for that night or even for that weekend, but for the next 80 years of their life.”

—Jay Giedd, Q&A, “Interview: Jay Giedd,” PBS, 2011. www.pbs.org.

Giedd is a neuroscientist at the National Institute of Mental Health.

“On the first night of Christmas break 2008, my daughter and her friends began drinking at a nearby home. It is unclear what happened, but we are told Shelby became violently ill and was semi-conscious when her friends left her propped up over the toilet. When she was discovered the next morning, she could not be revived.”

—Debbie Allen, “A Message from the Director,” Shelby's Rules, 2009. www.shelbysrulesfoundation.com.

Allen founded Shelby's Rules, a nonprofit organization dedicated to educating people about the dangers of binge drinking, after her daughter died of alcohol poisoning.

“[Leslie] . . . suffers from epilepsy as a direct result of her long-term alcohol and drug abuse. When Leslie fell during an epileptic seizure, she developed a hematoma that caused damage to her brain.”

—Boonshoft School of Medicine, “CAM Testimonials: Leslie's Story,” December 17, 2007.

Boonshoft School of Medicine's Consumer Advocacy Model (CAM) program assists people who are experiencing alcohol, drug, or mental health problems.

“Teenage alcoholism often starts with teenage drinking . . . at social events and may end up costing your teen’s life or someone else’s life if a drinking and driving accident occurs.”

—Sarita Uhr, “Teenage Alcoholism: Stop Teenage Drinking and Driving Now!,” Teenage Alcoholism.net, January 12, 2011. http://teenagealcoholism.net.

Uhr is a psychiatrist, writer, and speaker who treats those with addiction problems.

“What stood out for me . . . was how frequently violence was a contributor to, or outcome of, the substance use. For some, the violence occurred prior to the underage drinking and for others the violence occurred while either one or both the victim and offender were under the influence of alcohol.”

—Susan Dreher, “Underage Drinking: Reason to Care,” *Brunswick (ME) Times Record*, September 24, 2010. www.timesrecord.com.

Dreher, executive director of Sexual Assault Support Services of Midcoast Maine in Brunswick, writing about her experiences when she worked at a substance-abuse prevention and treatment program for adolescents.

“The evidence is consistent that [the earlier] underage drinking occurs, the higher the number of suicide thoughts and suicide attempts in older adolescents.”

—Sarita Uhr, “Early Drinking, Early Dying! Teenage Suicide Risk,” Teenage Alcoholism.net, October 16, 2010. http://teenagealcoholism.net.

Uhr is a psychiatrist, writer, and speaker who treats those with addiction problems.

Facts and Illustrations

What Are the Dangers of Teenage Alcoholism?

- In 2008 the Drug Abuse Warning Network found that **188,981** alcohol-related emergency room visits were made by patients aged 12 to 20, accounting for **32.9 percent** of all drug-related visits made by this age group.
- According to the CDC, excessive alcohol consumption contributes to more than **4,600 deaths** among underage youth (less than 21 years of age) in the United States each year.
- **Zero-tolerance** laws in all states make it illegal for youth under age 21 to drive with any measurable amount of alcohol in their systems.
- In 2009, **10 percent** of high school students reported driving a car or other vehicle during the past 30 days when they had been drinking alcohol.
- In 2009 a New York City Health Department survey found that condom use was less common **(63 percent)** among teens who reported using alcohol or drugs before sex than among those who were sober **(72 percent)**.
- When asked whether teens they know who drink alcohol or use illegal drugs are more likely to engage in **sexual activity**, three out of four teens said "yes" in the 2010 *National Survey of American Attitudes on Substance Abuse XV: Teens and Parents.*

Teen Drinking Affects Grades

Studies have shown that teens who drink get lower grades than teens who do not drink. A 2010 report from the Office of National Drug Control Policy shows that a much lower percentage of students who typically get As and Bs drink compared with those who get Cs, Ds, and Fs.

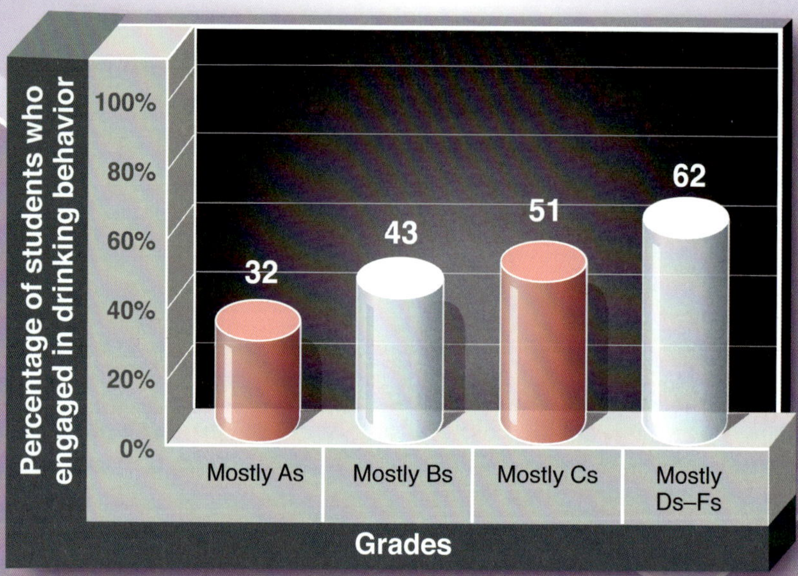

Source: Office of National Drug Control Policy, "Back to School," August 2010. www.whitehousedrugpolicy.gov.

- SAMHSA found in 2008 that **13 percent** of teenagers with significant behavioral problems also were dependent on alcohol.
- A 2008 study by Georgia State University professor Monica Swahn found that teens who begin drinking at a young age are three times more likely than nondrinking peers to attempt **suicide**.

Dangerous Effects of Alcohol on Teens

Alcohol adversely affects a teenager's body, mind, and emotions. The potential effects of drinking include impaired judgment, coordination, and ability to react. The effects in these and other areas worsen as the alcohol intake increases.

	Mental	Physical	Emotional
1–3 Drinks	• Judgment • Concentration	• Coordination	• Happy and feel good
2–8 Drinks	• Reasoning • Reaction Time • Unconsciousness	• Reaction Time • Severe Motor Impairment • Unconsciousness	• Disinhibited/Loud • Mood Swings • Stupor
7–8 Drinks	• Death	• Breathing • Heart • Bladder • Death	• Unconsciousness • Death

Source: Aimee L. Stern, *Delaying That First Drink: A Parent's Guide*, American Association for Advancement of Science, 2010. www.sciencenetlinks.com.

- The CDC 2009 *Youth Risk Behavior Survey* found that among the **34.2 percent** of sexually active students nationwide, **21.6 percent** had drunk alcohol or used drugs before last engaging in sexual intercourse.

- Of 4,271 students surveyed at more than 10 North Carolina universities, **one-fourth** who had had a drink in the previous 30 days had mixed alcohol with **energy drinks**, according to researchers at Wake Forest University School of Medicine in North Carolina. Additionally, they got drunk twice as often and drank more per session than those who had alcohol without caffeine.

Fatalities Involving Young Alcohol-Impaired Drivers

In the United States in 2009, according to a report issued by the distillers industry group The Century Council, 1,398 people died in car crashes involving at least one alcohol-impaired driver under the age of 21. The map shows the number of deaths by state.

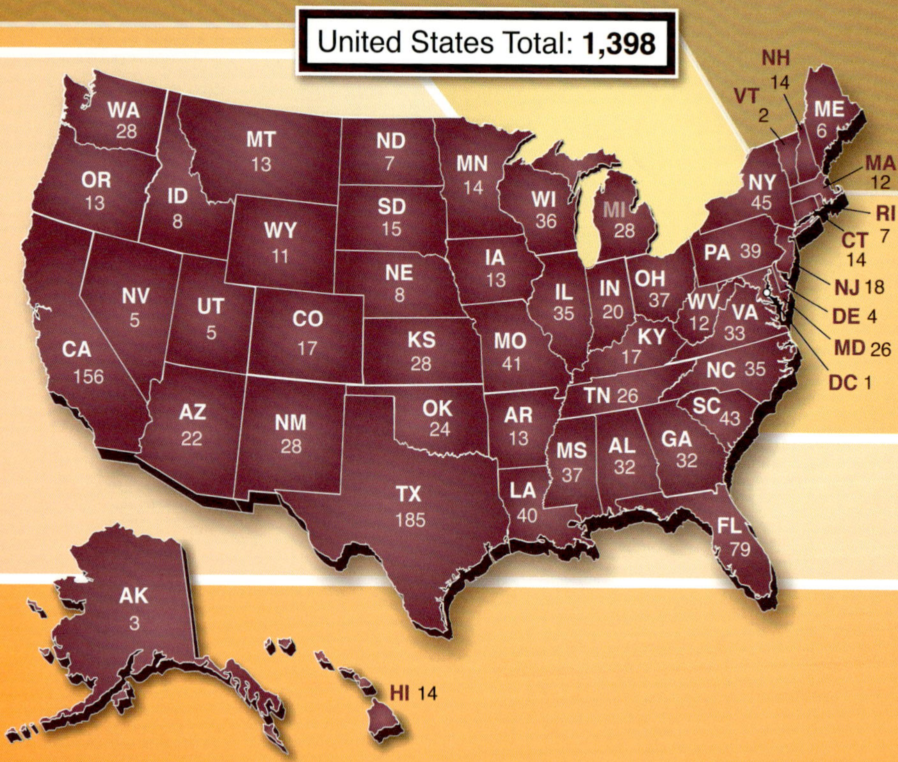

Source: Century Council 2009, *State of Drunk Driving Fatalities in the United States*, 2009. www.centurycouncil.org.

- According to the National Foundation for Suicide Prevention, alcoholism is a factor in about **30 percent** of all **completed suicides**, including those involving teenagers.

How Is Teenage Alcoholism Treated?

“Getting kids into treatment sooner, making sure they complete it and re-intervening as soon as possible after relapse significantly reduces how long it takes to get them to stable recovery.”

—Michael Dennis, senior research psychologist at Chestnut Health Systems in Bloomington, Illinois.

“Alcohol and drug rehab programs for teens are the best solution for young people who are unable to stop taking drugs or drinking alcohol, and have seen their family lives and schoolwork suffer as a result.”

—Michael's House, an addiction treatment center in Palm Springs, California.

According to the *National Survey on Drug Use and Health*, 1.2 million people (4.8 percent of the youth population) aged 12 to 17 needed treatment for an alcohol problem in 2009. Alcoholism treatment is available in many different forms—residential treatment centers, outpatient treatment centers, group counseling, family counseling, self-help groups, and therapy. However, teens generally need treatment that has been tailored specially for them because teenage alcoholics have different needs than adult alcoholics.

> **Experts say that having support from and open communication with parents or guardians is essential to remaining sober.**

One important aspect of treating teens is improving their relations with family members. Family counseling is typically included in treatment programs for teens because most teens live with their families. Experts say that having support from and open communication with parents or guardians is essential to remaining sober.

Other components of treatment for teenage alcoholics concern school and friends. Any program for teens must include a way to keep up with their education during treatment. And because young people are likely to continue seeing the same kids at school and at home, alcoholic teens must be taught how to deal with peer pressure.

There are treatment programs throughout the United States that meet the specific needs of adolescents. These programs include inpatient and outpatient care along with counseling programs. However, not all alcoholic teens in need have access to youth treatment programs.

Not Getting Treatment

Based on the *National Survey on Drug Use and Health,* only 96,000 of the alcoholic youth who needed treatment received it at a hospital, inpatient treatment center, outpatient treatment center, or mental health facility. This left almost 1.1 million youth who needed but did not receive treatment at any of these types of facilities. These teenagers either received no treatment of any kind or sought treatment through programs such as Alcoholics Anonymous (AA).

Many teens do not get treatment because of the cost; parents or guardians who do not have health insurance may not be able to afford treatment. Inpatient treatment programs can be extremely expensive; one well-known facility for young people charges up to $28,000 a month. Even outpatient programs can be expensive; the typical youth outpatient program at the same facility costs $8,900 to attend four sessions a week for eight weeks.

While cost is an obstacle for many teens, actually finding a treatment program specifically designed for teenage alcoholics may be an even greater obstacle. Few such programs exist, and those that do usually have long waiting lists. According to the 2008 *National Survey of Substance Abuse Treatment Services*, only one-third of substance abuse programs in the United States offer specialized programs for teens.

Involuntary Treatment

The average teenage alcoholic starts treatment only after someone—family members, school officials, or the judicial system—forces them into it. This is known as involuntary treatment. A teen who involuntarily enters a treatment program often has not reached the point of acknowledging that he or she has a problem, or the teen might think it is possible to conquer the problem without any help.

Interestingly, some studies show that people who enter treatment involuntarily have the same success rates as those who choose to get treatment. One study by University of California at Los Angeles researchers found that treatment outcomes were basically the same for methamphetamine addicts required by a judge to enter treatment and addicts who sought treatment on their own. This and other studies indicate that once a person is actually in treatment, the way he or she got there is not relevant once that person recognizes the problem.

> **"A teen who involuntarily enters a treatment program often has not reached the point of acknowledging that he or she has a problem."**

Like many alcoholic teens, Shawn was forced into treatment. She began drinking and taking drugs at age 10, and this use spiraled out of control. In 2004, when she was 18, Shawn's mom told her she could either enter a treatment center or leave the house. Having nowhere else to go, Shawn reluctantly chose treatment. "At first, I really didn't want to be clean and free from drugs and alcohol," writes Shawn as a testimonial for the program she attended at Treatment Solutions of South Florida. "I kicked and screamed all the way through but Treatment Solutions never gave up on me. . . . God willing, I will celebrate 6 years clean on January 24th 2011."[18]

Outpatient Treatment Centers

Outpatient treatment centers are a typical choice for teen alcoholics. At outpatient centers teens can get treatment but still continue to go to school and live with their families. According to the 2008 *National Survey of Substance Abuse Treatment Centers*, 88 percent of substance abusers aged 18 and younger who received treatment attended outpatient centers.

Visions, in Los Angeles, California, is a typical adolescent outpatient treatment program. During the first phase of the year-long program, teens attend four counseling sessions weekly where they identify what causes them to drink or take drugs and learn about the 12 steps, a set of steps developed by AA that addicts follow to remain sober. In the second phase, teens continue to meet twice a week to work on how to prevent a relapse. During the last six months of the program, the teens attend weekly peer group meetings for ongoing support to remain sober. Throughout the program, family members take part in counseling in order to develop good family communication skills and solid relationships.

Residential Treatment Centers

A residential treatment program is an option for a teen alcoholic who needs a more intensive program than an outpatient program provides. At residential centers, teens live on-site under constant supervision, allowing them to immerse themselves in the program. The 2008 *National Survey of Substance Abuse Treatment Services* found that 11 percent of adolescents who attended substance abuse treatment programs received treatment at residential treatment centers.

One of these centers, the Newport Academy, requires a minimum stay of 45 days and provides a full schedule for its patients during this time. A typical day includes individual therapy, group therapy, life skills classes, and tutoring so that they do not fall behind in school. A unique part of the program includes equine therapy, which is where the teens work with horses, both caring for and riding them. The purpose of equine therapy is to give youth a sense of responsibility and a way to focus on something other than themselves. "Therapists say that young people who ordinarily shun physical and emotional closeness with other people can often accept it from a horse," states the Equine Therapy website. "The child-horse bond can develop mutual trust, respect, affection, empathy, unconditional acceptance, confidence, responsibility, assertiveness, communication skills and self-control."[19]

Mixed Views on Group Therapy

Most treatment programs for teenage alcoholics rely heavily on group therapy with addicts of similar ages. Some mental health professionals believe that group settings with positive peer pressure will help teen addicts make good choices in their lives because peer influences are important to teenagers. "[Teens in group therapy] realize they are not odd or weird because they have problems. Other adolescents have the same problems," writes Michelle Bolyn, a therapist. "When there is a group of teenagers who struggle with similar issues, it helps to make the group more cohesive. They relate to each other and learn to support each other."[20]

> **At residential centers, teens live on-site under constant supervision, allowing them to immerse themselves in the program.**

Other professionals disagree. They believe that group therapy encourages users to keep using. "I've known kids who have gone into inpatient treatment and met other users. After treatment, they meet up with them and explore new drugs and become more seriously involved in drug use,"[21] says Tom Dishion, director of research at the Child and Family Center at the University of Oregon, who has documented such peer influence in scientific studies. Dishion and others believe that teen substance abusers who spend a lot of time together during treatment actually encourage continued alcohol or drug use.

Do Medications Help?

Doctors can prescribe medications to help alcoholics stop drinking, but the three main medications, disulfiram, naltrexone, and acamprosate, are only available to people aged 18 and over. So older teenagers might benefit from them, but younger teenagers will not. The age restriction on these drugs is a result of studies of how the drugs work. The US Food and Drug Administration (FDA) conducted such studies only on adults because many more adults than teenagers are in need of the drugs.

Used by alcoholics for over 50 years, disulfiram, also known as Antabuse, works by making a person feel sick if they drink alcohol. It is the most common medication used by alcoholics, with approximately 200,000 people using it daily. A 2006 study tracked alcoholics who had taken disulfiram for over 9 years and found a 52 percent abstinence rate among its users. With the relapse rate for alcoholics at about 60 percent, this figure is considered a relative success. Another positive feature of disulfiram is that the side effects such as a metallic taste in the mouth and headaches are typically mild.

"Relapse is common among alcoholics of all ages."

The drug naltrexone was approved by the FDA in 1994 as a daily oral medication. Subsequently, the FDA approved an injectable monthly dose of naltrexone in 2006. This medication works by reducing the craving for alcohol. It achieves this by blocking activity in the brain's reward system, which is thought to play a central role in alcohol dependence. Initial studies found that alcoholics who used naltrexone achieved a 51 percent abstinence rate versus only 23 percent for those who took placebos in the studies. Its popularity is increasing due both to the reduction of cravings and the fact that its side effects are relatively minor, mainly consisting of nausea.

A different type of medication to help alcoholics is acamprosate. This medication reduces anxiety in alcoholics who no longer drink. Years of drinking large amounts of alcohol can disrupt the way a person's brain works, resulting in anxiety and insomnia. This medication helps stabilize the chemical balance in the brain to reduce extreme anxiety and insomnia in recovering alcoholics.

These drugs can be useful tools to help older teenagers and adults who are trying to remain sober. However, medications are not considered a cure for alcoholism; health professionals recommend that all alcoholics, no matter what their age, get involved in treatment programs that help people emotionally break their dependence on alcohol.

Support After Recovery

Once teens have completed treatment for alcoholism their journey is not over. Relapse is common among alcoholics of all ages with various studies finding that between 60 and 90 percent of alcoholics relapse. For this reason, health professionals agree that aftercare following treatment is a necessity to stay sober.

Aftercare treatment comes in different forms. AA, one of the most well known such programs, is a mutual support program for recovering alcoholics. Members attend regular meetings with other alcoholics and are assigned a sponsor to help them maintain sobriety. Proponents of AA claim that these meetings can help alcoholic teenagers learn to deal with life problems without returning to alcohol. However, some believe that AA can actually harm teenage alcoholics because they must admit they have no control over alcohol without the help of a higher being. This may lead teens, particularly those who are unsure if they believe in a higher being, to think they have no chance of staying sober.

Maintaining sobriety after treatment can also be achieved at sober schools, private schools that include alcohol and drug addiction counseling and classes in their curricula. Kayla Causey, at 16, decided to attend Oklahoma Outreach Sober School after completing a treatment program for her alcoholism. "I get my schoolwork done easier and with less stress, without having to worry about people under-the-influence around me," Kayla said. "I definitely think this is going to give me a good foundation to go off of, once I get out of school."[22] Having received treatment and aftercare, Kayla has increased her chances for living a sober life. Any teenage alcoholic who does the same has the chance of living a fulfilling life and maintaining sobriety.

Primary Source Quotes*

How Is Teenage Alcoholism Treated?

“Outpatient treatment centers are great for a teenager that is willing to admit that they have a problem and want some help in treating it. This includes AA meetings as well as a lot of therapy, whether it be group, family or individual. This type of treatment is one of the most popular among teenagers.”

—Teen Alcohol Rehab, “Teen Alcohol Rehab Explained,” 2011. http://teenalcoholrehab.net.

Teen Alcohol Rehab is a website that was designed to provide information about teen drug and alcohol addiction and the treatments available.

“[Teen substance abusers] are much more likely to be coerced by their parents, their schools and/or the court or social services system to enter treatment. While treatment does not need to be voluntary to be effective, special consideration needs to be given to these issues as part of the adolescent’s treatment.”

—Thomas J. Crowley and Elizabeth Whitmore, “Why Adolescent Treatment Is Different than Adult Treatment,” HBO, 2011. www.hbo.com.

Crowley and Whitmore are both medical professionals with expertise in substance abuse.

* Editor’s Note: While the definition of a primary source can be narrowly or broadly defined, for the purposes of Compact Research, a primary source consists of: 1) results of original research presented by an organization or researcher; 2) eyewitness accounts of events, personal experience, or work experience; 3) first-person editorials offering pundits’ opinions; 4) government officials presenting political plans and/or policies; 5) representatives of organizations presenting testimony or policy.

"Oftentimes one of the biggest challenges in treating young people with substance abuse problems is getting them to accept that they might actually have a problem; teens and adolescents haven't usually hit a "bottom" as devastating as that experienced by lifelong addicts."

—Sarah Michaels, "Drug Rehab—Does Hollywood Glamorize Drug Addiction?," Drug Rehab—Stop Addiction, June 23, 2010. http://drugcure.net.

Michaels is the general manager of Cirque Lodge, a drug rehab and addiction treatment facility located in Sundance, Utah.

"Inpatient treatment centers are for those teenagers that are highly addicted to drinking and have been for a while and will need medical attention while they are getting all of the alcohol out of their system."

—Teen Alcohol Rehab, "Teen Alcohol Rehab Explained," 2011. http://teenalcoholrehab.net.

Teen Alcohol Rehab is a website that was designed to provide information about teen drug and alcohol addiction and the treatments available.

"In my opinion, 90 days should be the minimum number of days for a teen or young adult to go to treatment. The longer programs seem to have better results."

—Sarita Uhr, "Do Rehab Centers for Teenage Alcoholism/Drug Abuse Even Work?," Teenage Alcoholism, January 22, 2011. http://teenagealcoholism.net.

Uhr is a psychiatrist, writer, and speaker who treats those with addiction problems.

"Most teenagers are more likely to take advice from a peer than an adult. A teen's therapist can tell him that he should cut back on his drug use, because he's putting his life in danger, but he's more likely to hear and take the advice if it comes from a peer."

—Michelle Bolyn, "Adolescent Group Therapy Benefits," Livestrong, January 26, 2010. www.livestrong.com.

Bolyn is a licensed mental health professional.

"For many people, true recovery that 'sticks' doesn't come until after the addict has attended an alcohol treatment program two or three times over the course of years."

—Newport Academy, "Teen Alcohol Treatment Tips," 2010. www.newport-academy.com.

The Newport Academy is an adolescent substance abuse treatment center.

Facts and Illustrations

How Is Teenage Alcoholism Treated?

- The 2009 *National Survey of Drug Use and Health* reports that **96,000** youth who were dependent on alcohol received treatment for alcohol abuse at a specialty facility.
- The 2008 *National Survey of Substance Abuse Treatment Centers* found that youth under age 18 made up **7 to 8 percent** of all clients at substance abuse treatment centers.
- According to the 2008 *National Survey of Substance Abuse Treatment Services*, only **one-third** of substance abuse programs in the United States offer specialized programs for teens.
- Hazelton, a renowned substance abuse treatment center, estimates the cost for an adolescent attending its outpatient treatment program in Minnesota to be **$589** per day.
- Hazelton estimates the cost for adolescents attending its residential treatment program in Minnesota to be **$877** per day.
- The 2009 *National Survey on Drug Use and Health* reports that approximately **1.1 million** youths needed but did not receive alcohol abuse treatment.
- According to the 2008 *National Survey of Substance Abuse Treatment Centers*, **88 percent** of substance abusers aged 18 and younger attended outpatient centers.

Teen Participation in Alcoholics Anonymous

Alcoholics Anonymous (AA), well known worldwide for helping alcoholics achieve and maintain sobriety, does not have a specific program for teenage alcoholics. Nevertheless, many teens do seek help from AA although they represent a small percentage of the organization's overall membership numbers.

Percentage of Members

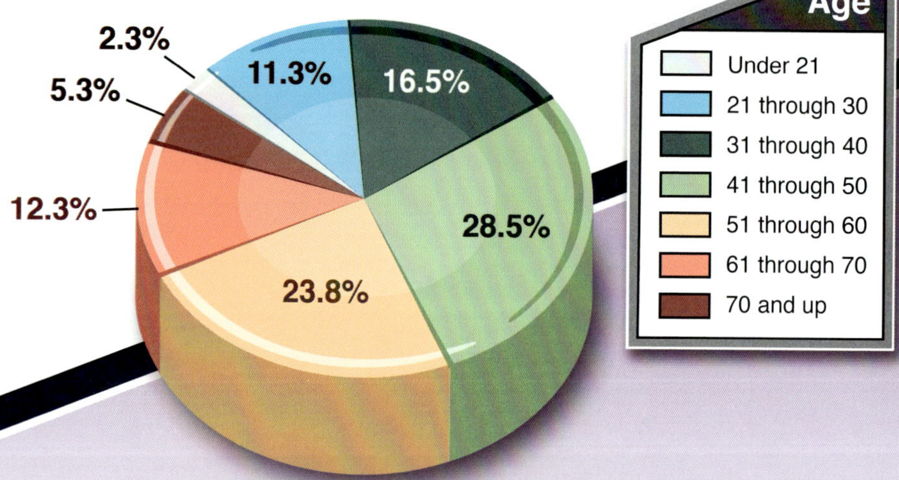

Source: *Alcoholics Anonymous 2007 Membership Survey*, A.A. Grapevine Inc., 2007. www.aa.org.

- A 2008 study by Harvard Medical School found that teenagers who followed up residential treatment with either **Alcoholics Anonymous** or **Narcotics Anonymous** for at least 6 months were more likely to remain abstinent over time than those who did not attend follow-up meetings.

- Approximately **10 percent** of Alcoholics Anonymous members are under age 30.

Most Teen Alcoholics Get Outpatient Treatment

Substance abuse programs for teenagers, which usually address both alcohol and drug dependency, are generally divided into three categories: outpatient, residential, and hospital inpatient. Of 86,465 young people getting treatment in one of these programs in 2008, by far the largest number took part in outpatient programs.

Type of Treatment for Patients Under Age 18 in 2008

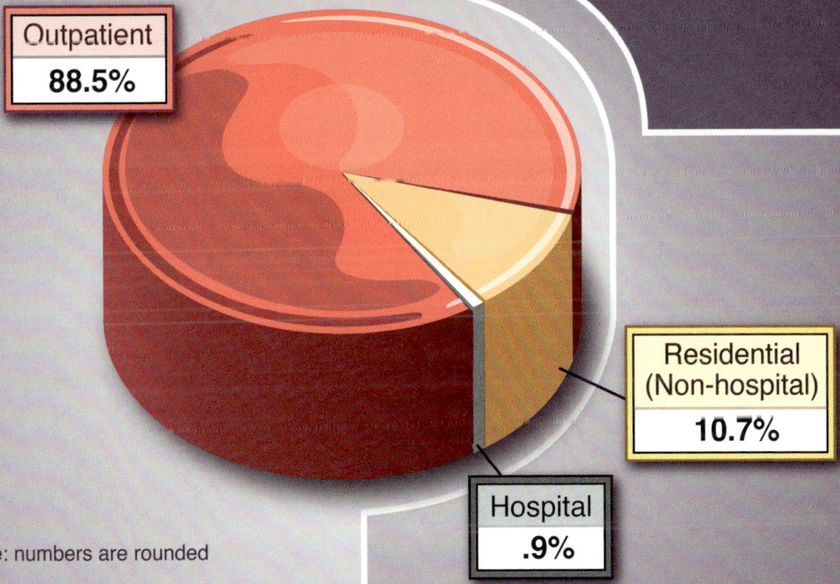

Note: numbers are rounded

Source: US Department of Health and Human Services, *National Survey on Substance Abuse Treatment Centers*, 2008. www.samhsa.gov.

- The first step of the **AA** 12-step program is, "We admitted we were powerless over alcohol—that our lives had become unmanageable."
- **Sober schools**, also known as recovery schools, are high schools that combine a high school curriculum along with recovery support services and a typical 12-step model of recovery.

Treatment Programs for Specific Populations

Some alcoholism treatment programs target the unique needs of specific populations. Adolescents, people with HIV or AIDS, and pregnant women are among those who can benefit from targeted programs. However, many centers do not offer such programs and those that do are usually very expensive.

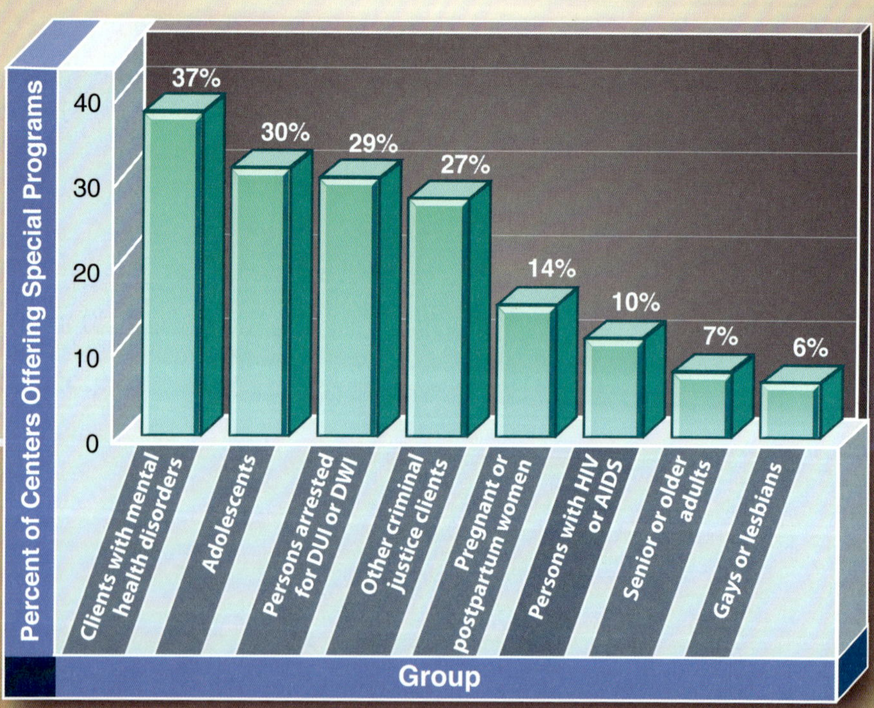

Source: US Department of Health and Human Services, *National Survey on Substance Abuse Treatment Centers*, 2008. www.samhsa.gov.

- In 2008, according to the Drug Abuse Warning Network, approximately one in five **(19.1 percent)** of 12- to 20-year-olds who were admitted to the emergency departments of hospitals for alcohol-related problems received some sort of substance abuse treatment, such as counseling or a treatment program, after being released.

Can Teenage Alcoholism Be Prevented?

"If I could wave a magic wand to make a dent in our nation's substance abuse problem, I would make sure that every child in America had dinner with his or her parents at least five times a week."

—Joseph A. Califano Jr., founder and chairman of the National Center on Addiction and Substance Abuse at Columbia University.

"Parent Disapproval is the Number One reason children choose not to drink alcohol. Parents empowered can trump peer pressure."

—Virginia Governor's Office for Substance Abuse Prevention, 2010.

Experts say the best way to prevent teenage alcoholism is for young people to delay drinking until they are older. Data from the National Longitudinal Alcohol Epidemiologic Studies show that 40.6 percent of people who first tried alcohol when they were 12 years old or younger became dependent on alcohol. For those who waited to drink alcohol until they were older, dependence rates were significantly lower. Only 16.6 percent of those who waited until age 18 to drink became dependent on alcohol and even less, 10.6 percent, of those who waited until age 21 to drink became dependent.

Convincing teenagers to not drink is made more difficult by the prevalence of alcohol in social settings. One way to encourage teens to think twice about drinking is to have them take part in prevention programs at school and in community groups. These programs often promote ways for teens to have fun without alcohol and teach teens ways they can respond to friends if they are pressured to drink. Experts say the most effective way to prevent teens from drinking is for parents to talk to their teens about the dangers of drinking.

Parental Talks

Studies have shown that one of the best ways to prevent teen alcohol abuse is for parents to talk openly and honestly with their kids about alcohol use and its dangers. According to the Partnership for a Drug-Free America, kids who learn about the risks of drugs and alcohol from their parents are up to 50 percent less likely to use these substances than those whose parents do not address the issue. Also, even if teens have experimented with alcohol, their parents can still prevent them from continuing to drink by talking with them. "The earlier parents take action to address a child's drug or alcohol use, the greater the chance they'll be effective in preventing a serious problem,"[23] states Ken C. Winters, an expert on adolescent substance abuse.

> **"Convincing teenagers to not drink is made more difficult by the prevalence of alcohol in social settings."**

Despite the evidence that talking to youth helps prevent alcohol use, in 2009, according to the *National Survey on Drug Use and Health*, only 58.2 percent of youths aged 12 to 17 reported that they had talked at least once with at least one of their parents about the dangers of drug, tobacco, or alcohol use. One reason for this is that many parents feel they do not know what to say or how to say it. According to 2010 data from the Partnership at Drugfree and MetLife Foundation, more than one in five parents feel unable to prevent their kids from trying drugs and alcohol.

A relatively easy way for parents to help prevent their teens from drinking is to have family dinners during which parents and teens have an opportunity to talk about topics such as alcohol. Studies show that teens from families that routinely eat dinner together are less likely to experiment with alcohol than teens from families that do not eat together. A 2009 study by the National Center on Addiction and Substance Abuse (CASA) at Columbia University found that teenagers who do not eat dinner with their families five to seven times per week are twice as likely to have used alcohol than those who do eat with their family five to seven times per week. According to Joseph A. Califano Jr., the founder and chairman of CASA, "America's drug problem is not going to be solved in courtrooms or legislative hearing rooms by judges and politicians. It will be solved in living rooms and dining rooms and across kitchen tables—by parents and families."[24]

"Strong relationships between parents and children have been shown to decrease the likelihood of a teen drinking."

Counseling and Therapy

Addressing any type of personal or family problem through counseling can prevent teens from becoming dependent on alcohol. When teens deal with difficult issues, such as depression or divorce, they may turn to alcohol as an escape if they have no other way of handling these stresses. Dealing with these problems professionally, early on, can prevent a teenager from turning to alcohol.

Most family issues can be addressed through family therapy, where teens and their parents attend counseling sessions together. Family therapy can help teens develop better communication and stronger ties with their parents. Strong relationships between parents and children have been shown to decrease the likelihood of teen drinking.

Untreated, mental health issues such as depression can lead to alcoholism and other addictive behaviors. Through therapy with mental health professionals, teens can learn to handle the emotional problems in their lives. As a result, they develop ways to deal with problems without needing alcohol as an escape.

Even brief therapy and counseling has been found to reduce alcohol misuse among teens. One study found that teens who had been admitted to a Flint, Michigan, emergency room and had been involved in violence and alcohol misuse in the past year benefited from a single 30-minute therapy intervention. The study, conducted at the emergency department from September 2006 to September 2009, randomly assigned the teens to one of three groups. The first group of teens talked with a therapist. The second group answered questions on a computer about goals and reasons to avoid drinking. The third group received brochures with referrals to community resources. After three months, participants in the therapy group showed a 70 percent to 76 percent reduction in violence and a decrease in alcohol abuse when compared with the other two groups.

Extracurricular Activities

When teens participate in after-school activities that are supervised by adults they are less likely to drink alcohol and develop dependency problems. Studies show that teens who participate in activities between the hours of 3:00 p.m. and 7:00 p.m. are more likely to abstain from drugs, alcohol, or cigarettes than those without activities. Teens who are not in activities often find themselves unsupervised during this time period since it is after school and before many working parents come home. Research has found that many teens engage in risky behaviors such as abusing alcohol during this unstructured time.

According to Parents, The Anti-Drug, an online information source for parents sponsored by the National Youth Anti-Drug Media Campaign, nearly 20 percent of teens who were not involved in any after-school activities reported current use of illicit drugs, alcohol, and cigarettes compared with only 12 percent who were involved in one to three such activities. "In America today, millions of young people are alone and unsupervised in the hours after school, before parents return home from work," explains the After-School All-Stars website, an organization that provides after-school programs for kids, "This situation places children and teens at grave risk for juvenile crime, substance abuse, teen pregnancy, and other problems."[25]

Community and School Programs

Community and school prevention programs have been successful at preventing teen alcohol and drug abuse because they provide teens information about the dangers of substance use and teach teens how to respond to peer pressure. These programs are also successful at reaching a large number of teenagers. In 2009, according to the *National Survey on Drug Use and Health*, 74.9 percent of young people reported having seen a prevention program at school.

> **Research has found that many unstructured teens engage in risky behaviors such as abusing alcohol during unstructured time.**

SADD, Students Against Destructive Decisions, began over 30 years ago as a program in which young people lead the education and prevention initiatives in their schools and communities. Founded as Students Against Driving Drunk in 1981 in Wayland, Massachusetts, SADD has grown to become the nation's main peer-to-peer youth education and prevention organization, with thousands of chapters in middle schools, high schools, and colleges. It has evolved to fight not just against underage drinking but all types of destructive teen behavior.

Communities That Care is one of many community prevention programs that have been implemented across the United States. A dozen small and mid-size towns in seven states have employed this program, which was developed by youth social work specialists David Hawkins and Richard Catalano in 1992. In each Communities That Care location a confidential youth survey is given to students in the area's schools to identify the main risk factors for developing problem behaviors such as drinking. A coalition of local government leaders, school administrators, health professionals, and parents then use this information to determine how to reduce these risks. The coalition implements different strategies from the program such as student/adult mentor programs, family-strengthening classes, and education programs. Where it has been implemented, the program has reduced alcohol use by eighth graders by nearly a quarter and binge drinking by 37 percent, according to findings published in 2009 in *Archives of Pediatrics and Adolescent Medicine*.

Religious Affiliation Reduces Drinking

Teens who are in families that regularly attend religious services have been found to be less likely to experiment with alcohol than those who do not attend such services. The 2009 *National Survey of American Attitudes on Substance Abuse XV* found that teens who attend religious services at least four times a month are less likely to smoke, drink, or use marijuana than those who do not attend services.

> **Research shows that teens involved in spiritual and religious activities can overcome a genetic tendency for alcoholism.**

Other research shows that teens involved in spiritual and religious activities can overcome a genetic tendency for alcoholism. In 2010 the University of Colorado at Boulder reported its findings in a study that tracked 1,432 twin pairs who had family histories of alcohol abuse. The researchers found that "religiosity" exerted a strong enough influence over the behavior of adolescents to override their genetic tendency toward alcoholism. Twins who were nonreligious were much more influenced by genetic factors for problem alcohol use. "Our study showed that genetic factors could influence problem alcohol use more in nonreligious adolescents than adolescents with a greater religious outlook,"[26] said Tanya M.M. Button, a postdoctoral fellow at the University of Colorado at Boulder and one of the study's authors.

Social Host Laws

To prevent drunk driving and other risky behaviors, some parents believe it is better to let their kids and friends drink at home where they can oversee their drinking. However, experts believe this only encourages teenagers to drink at an earlier age, which, as studies have shown, can lead to increased abuse and addiction. To prevent parent-supervised teen drinking, legislators in many states have adopted laws prohibiting adults from serving or supplying alcohol to anyone under age 21. Under these laws, adults can be held responsible for the actions of teens who drink under their supervision and then become involved in accidents that result in injuries or deaths.

These laws, called social host laws, vary from state to state. In most cases adults who break these laws can be charged for medical bills and property damage caused by teens who drank while under their supervision. For example, in Massachusetts the law allows police to charge anyone who owns or controls a home if a minor is drinking there, even if the homeowner did not provide the alcohol. The crime is a misdemeanor, with a penalty of up to a year in jail and a $2,000 fine.

Instead of hosting supervised drinking parties, experts recommend that parents plan alcohol-free events to prevent teenage drinking. "Many youth are able to resist using alcohol or other drugs except at parties and other celebrations that offer easy access to illegal or restricted substances," states the National Crime Prevention Council. "These events frequently lead to tragedy."[27] The National Crime Prevention Council suggests that parents and schools host alcohol-free dances, parties, and other social events to give teens an alternative to drinking events.

These parties and other preventive measures are meant to keep teens from experimenting with alcohol. Those who begin drinking early are more likely to become alcoholics. Those who wait have a better chance of developing into healthy, nonalcoholic adults.

Primary Source Quotes*

Can Teenage Alcoholism Be Prevented?

“Parents who sanction teenage drinking parties are making a huge mistake. These parents are encouraging the very behavior they are attempting to control.”

—William Damon, “Condoning Bad Behavior,” *Room for Debate, New York Times*, June 17, 2010. http://roomfordebate.blogs.nytimes.com.

Damon is a professor of education and the director of the Center on Adolescence at Stanford University.

“What is the problem with youthful drinking? It is children drinking in the woods, driving while drinking, developing unrealistic and escapist fantasies around alcohol, and the persistence of these problems into young adulthood and beyond. Sipping wine with parents at dinner or at religious ceremonies is the *antithesis* of a drinking problem.”

—Stanton Peele, “Would Legalization of Alcoholic Drinks to Minors Decrease or Increase Underage Drinking?,” The Stanton Peele Addiction Website, December 16, 2010. http://www.peele.net.

Peele is a psychologist who has been publishing articles about addiction for over 40 years.

* Editor’s Note: While the definition of a primary source can be narrowly or broadly defined, for the purposes of Compact Research, a primary source consists of: 1) results of original research presented by an organization or researcher; 2) eyewitness accounts of events, personal experience, or work experience; 3) first-person editorials offering pundits’ opinions; 4) government officials presenting political plans and/or policies; 5) representatives of organizations presenting testimony or policy.

"Parents have tremendous influence on teens' decisions to not drink and use drugs."

—Partnership at Drugfree.org, "Time to Talk," 2011. www.timetotalk.org.

The Partnership at Drugfree.org is a nonprofit organization that helps parents prevent, intervene in, and find treatment for drug and alcohol use by their children.

"Teen perceptions of parental disapproval are great deterrents: What parents may not realize is that children say parental disapproval of underage drinking is the key reason they have chosen not to drink."

—Virginia Governor's Office for Substance Abuse Prevention, *Underage Drinking*, 2010.

The Virginia Governor's Office for Substance Abuse Prevention is dedicated to preventing underage drinking in the state of Virginia.

"Students that come home to an unsupervised house after school will find ways to keep themselves busy, often having to do with drug or alcohol abuse. Teens that go to practice, drama club, or other structured activity are much less likely to get involved with drugs."

—Bethany Winkel, "Keep Kids Busy," Treatment Solutions Network, October 8, 2010. www.treatmentsolutionsnetwork.com.

Winkel has held the position of development coordinator for a nonprofit youth center for many years.

"If you are the parents of teens or children about to become teens, there is something that you can do that will greatly reduce their chances of becoming involved in alcohol and drugs: take them to church."

—Buddy T., "Take Teens to Church to Prevent Underage Drinking," About.com, July 15, 2010. http://alcoholism.about.com.

Buddy T. has been in recovery from alcoholism since July 1989 and has been the alcoholism guide for Yahoo! since February 1997.

"On Stand Out from the Crowd Day, students wear goofy clothes to show they don't blend into the background with drugs, alcohol, and other destructive decisions. Instead, they choose to stand out from that crowd and fight things that could harm them."

—SADD, "*Decisions*," Winter 2009.

SADD is a national nonprofit peer-led organization with the goal of keeping teens from making destructive decisions.

"To more effectively reach students, prevention professionals should begin to leverage new channels—using Facebook for Alcohol Awareness Week, Tweeting about alcohol-free options, doing peer education through online forums, using text messaging for enforcement at high-risk events, and so forth."

—Outside the Classroom, "The Future of Alcohol Prevention: Navigating Changes in the Higher Education Landscape," November 2010. www.outsidetheclassroom.com.

Outside the Classroom is a nationwide leader in alcohol prevention research and program development.

Can Teenage Alcoholism Be Prevented?

- According to 2010 data from the Partnership at Drugfree.org and MetLife Foundation, more than **one in five** parents feel unable to prevent their kids from trying drugs and alcohol.

- The Partnership at Drugfree.org reports that kids who learn about the risks of drugs and alcohol from their parents are up to **50 percent** less likely to use than those who do not.

- In 2009, according to the *National Survey on Drug Use and Health*, only **58.2 percent** of youths aged 12 to 17 reported that in the past year they had talked at least once with at least one parent about the dangers of drug, tobacco, or alcohol use.

- The National Center on Addiction and Substance Abuse at Columbia University found in 2009 that teens who say they **eat dinner with their families** at least five times a week are less likely to say they have friends who use alcohol, marijuana, tobacco, or someone else's prescription drugs.

- The National Center on Addiction and Substance Abuse at Columbia University found that **60 percent** of teens eat dinner with their families at least five times a week.

Where Teens Hear Prevention Messages

Preventing youth from experimenting with alcohol is the best way to keep them from developing an alcohol dependency. One significant way to accomplish this is to expose them to school and community alcohol prevention messages. The following chart shows the percentages of youth who report they have seen or heard prevention messages at school or through community programs. In both cases, a high percentage of students were exposed to these messages.

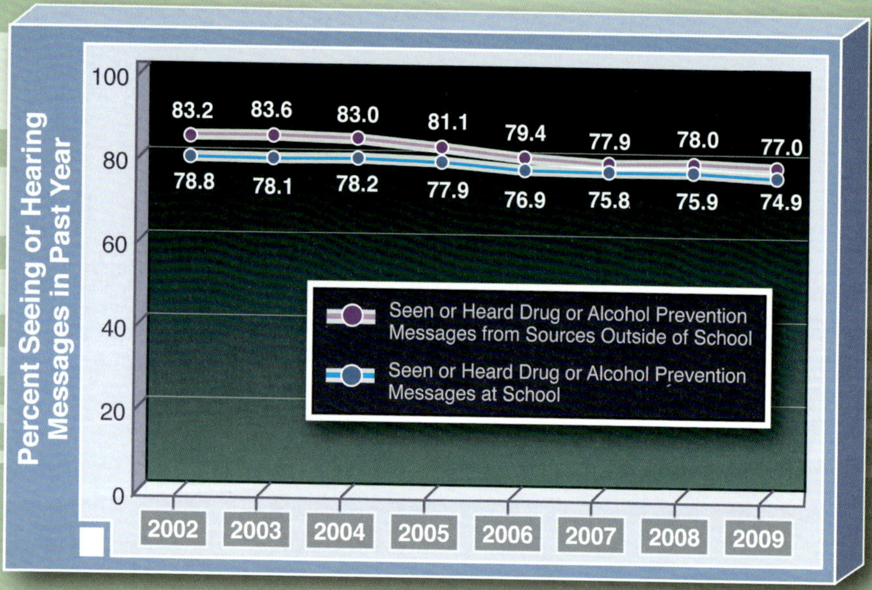

Source: US Department of Health and Human Services, *National Survey on Drug Use and Health*, 2009.

- According to the *2009 National Survey on Drug Use and Health*, approximately **one in eight youths aged 12 to 17** reported that they had participated in drug, tobacco, or alcohol prevention programs outside of school in the past year.

Popular Alcohol-Free Events

One way to prevent alcohol abuse by youth is to provide alcohol-free social events. A student survey in 2008 revealed that movie nights and live music were among the most popular alcohol-free events.

Students' Top-Ranked Alcohol-Free Options

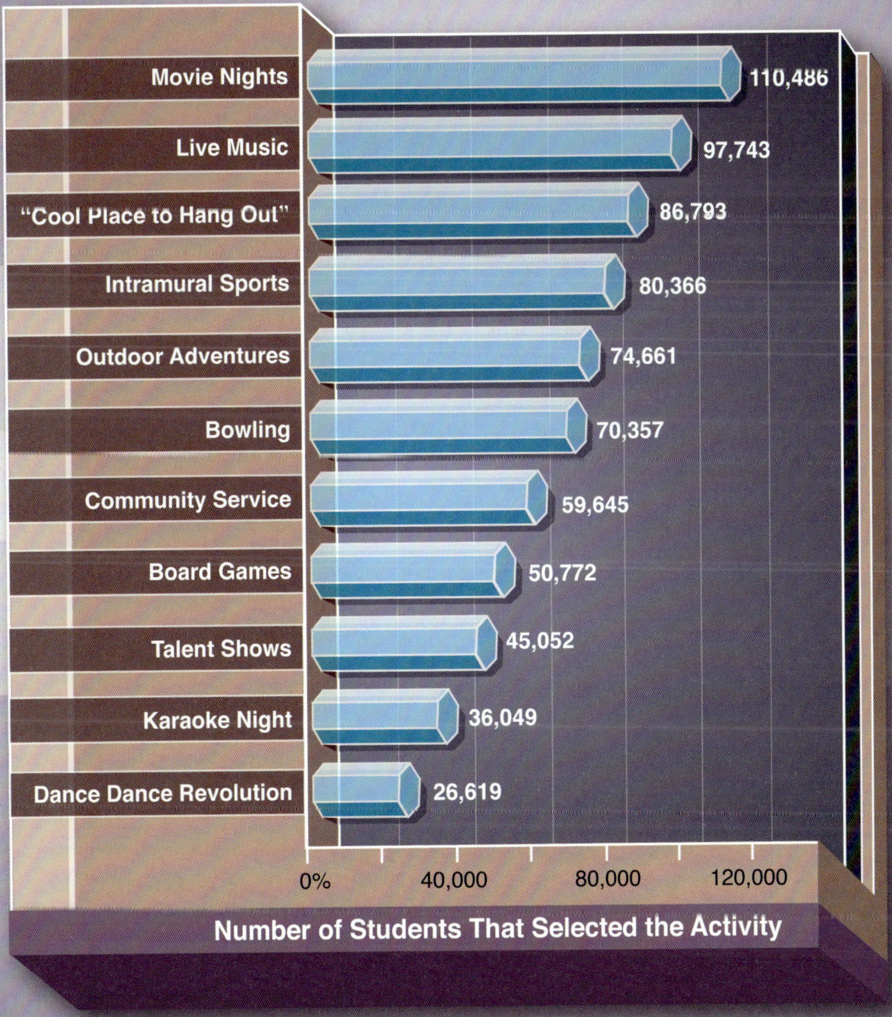

Source: Outside the Classroom, "Student Interest in Alcohol Free Events," 2008. www.outsidetheclassroom.com.

Strong Family Ties Prevent Alcohol Use

A 2010 survey found that teens with strong family ties are less likely to drink alcohol than teens with moderate to weak parental bonds.

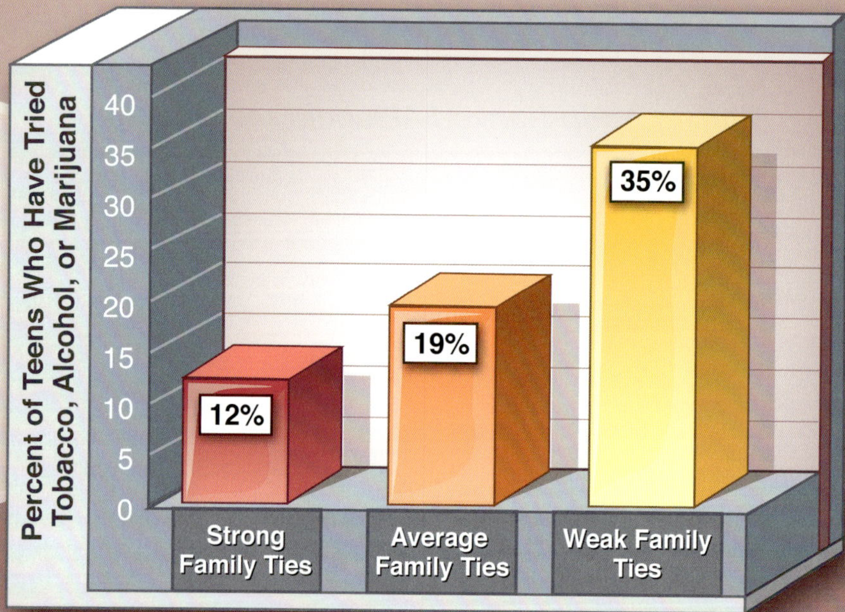

Source: National Center on Addiction and Substance Abuse at Columbia University, *National Survey of American Attitudes on Substance Abuse XV: Teens and Parents*, August 2010. www.casacolumbia.org.

- The *2009 National Survey on Drug Use and Health* found that **74.9 percent** of youths aged 12 to 17 enrolled in school reported that they had seen or heard drug or alcohol prevention messages at school in the past year.

- The **D.A.R.E.** program, a violence, drug, and alcohol prevention program used in schools for over 25 years, has tens of thousands of instructors throughout the United States and in 44 other countries.

- **SADD** reports that it has over **350,000** students that actively participate in the organization's chapters.
- The Communities That Care substance-abuse prevention program has reduced alcohol use by eighth graders by nearly a quarter and binge drinking by **37 percent**, according to findings reported in *Archives of Pediatrics and Adolescent Medicine* in 2009.
- In 2009 the *National Survey of American Attitudes on Substance Abuse XV* found that teens who attend **religious services** at least four times a month are four times less likely to smoke, drink, or use marijuana.
- A 2010 survey by the nationwide alcohol prevention organization Outside the Classroom found that the most popular alcohol free options among 500,000 college students are **movie nights and live music**.

Key People and Advocacy Groups

Alcoholics Anonymous: This nonprofit organization was established in 1935 and today has over 2 million members, both young and old. Its purpose is to provide alcoholics a free way to recover through meetings that follow a 12-step program.

Regina Benjamin: Benjamin is the current surgeon general of the United States. One of her duties is to prevent and reduce underage drinking.

Monique Bourgeois: Bourgeois is director of the Association of Recovery Schools. Its mission is to promote and expand recovery programs in secondary schools so teens in substance abuse recovery have a supportive place to attend school.

Leadership to Keep Children Alcohol Free: This organization is a coalition of current and former governors' spouses, federal agencies, and public and private organizations, dedicated to preventing the use of alcohol by young people between the ages of 9 and 15.

National Youth Anti-Drug Media Campaign: The US Congress created the National Youth Anti-Drug Media Campaign in 1989 to prevent and reduce youth drug and alcohol use.

Outside the Classroom: This organization is dedicated to providing students and schools across the nation with the information and tools they need to develop cost-effective strategies for reducing alcohol-related risk and preventing harm.

Stephen J. Pasierb: Pasierb is the chief executive officer and president of the Partnership at Drugfree.org. He has led the organization since 2001 in the effort to help parents prevent drug and alcohol use by their children.

Students Against Destructive Decisions (SADD): SADD, a non-profit organization, was formed over 30 years ago to fight against student drunk driving. Today, its mission includes providing students with the best possible prevention tools to deal with underage drinking, other drug use, impaired driving, and other destructive decisions.

Nora D. Volkow: Volkow became the director of the National Institute on Drug Abuse (NIDA) at the National Institutes of Health in 2003. As leader of NIDA, she runs programs that support research on the health aspects of alcohol and drug abuse and addiction, including specific studies on the effects of addiction on teens.

Chronology

1920
The prohibition on the manufacture, sale, and consumption of alcohol goes into effect in the United States.

1933
Prohibition ends in the United States.

1935
Bob Smith and Bill Wilson found Alcoholics Anonymous.

1953
The Yale Center of Alcohol Studies publishes a study of drinking habits among college students that finds that 79 percent of male drinkers and 65 percent of female drinkers had their first drink before starting college.

1975
Alabama lowers the state's legal age for purchasing alcohol from 21 to 19, following the trend of 29 other states that lowered drinking ages from 21 in the prior five years.

1981
Students Against Driving Drunk is founded in 1981 in Wayland, Massachusetts.

1983
D.A.R.E. is founded as a community and school substance-abuse and violence-prevention program.

1984
The US National Minimum Drinking Age is enacted and requires that all people who purchase and possess alcohol in public must be at least 21 years old.

1920 1955 1975 1985

1985 1990 1995 2000 2005 2010

1987
École Nouvelle in Minnesota opens as the nation's first sober high school, a high school for recovering teenage drug and alcohol addicts.

1992
March is established as National Drug and Alcohol Recovery Month to celebrate those who are recovering from drug and alcohol addiction.

1998
The US Congress creates the National Youth Anti-Drug Media Campaign to prevent and reduce youth drug and alcohol use.

2000
A study by the American Psychiatric Association finds that the the hippocampus (the area of the brain involved with learning and memory) in alcoholic youth is significantly smaller than in those who do not drink.

2006
In the United States the injectable form of naltrexone, which blocks the effects of alcohol, is approved by the FDA to treat alcohol dependence.

2007
Youth in the United States aged 12 to 17 who need treatment for an alcohol use problem number 1.4 million.

2008
Over 100 college presidents sign a petition urging lawmakers to lower the drinking age, claiming the 21-year-old drinking age has led to a culture of binge drinking on college campuses.

2010
President Barack Obama declares September 27, 2010, as Family Day, a day to join together by spending time with families as a way to help steer young people away from drugs and alcohol.

2011
Alaska state represesntative Bob Lynn introduces a bill that would allow military members under 21 to legally drink and smoke in his state.

Related Organizations

After-School All-Stars

9255 Sunset Blvd., Suite 500
Los Angeles, CA 90069
phone: (310) 275-3232 • fax: (310) 275-3230
website: www.afterschoolallstars.org

After-School All-Stars is a nationwide organization that provides after-school programs and activities for children and teens to keep them safe and away from drugs, alcohol, crime, and gangs. This organization promotes activities and ongoing relationships that increase confidence and encourage success.

American Academy of Child & Adolescent Psychiatry (AACAP)

3615 Wisconsin Ave. NW
Washington, DC 20016-3007
phone: (202) 966-7300 • fax: (202) 966-2891
e-mail: communications@aacap.org • website: http://aacap.org

AACAP is a nonprofit professional medical association dedicated to improving the quality of life for children and adolescents affected by mental, behavioral, or developmental disorders. One of its goals is to educate people about the consequences of teen substance abuse.

The Century Council

2345 Crystal Dr., Suite 910
Arlington, VA 22202
phone: (202) 637-0077
website: www.centurycouncil.org

The Century Council is an organization created by the distilled spirits industry. It supports programs aimed at reducing drunk driving and underage drinking.

The Courage to Speak Foundation

PO Box 1527
Norwalk, CT 06852
phone: (877) 431-3295
website: www.couragetospeak.org

This organization was founded in 1996 after the founders, Ginger and Larry Katz, lost their son to a drug overdose. Its mission is to incorporate drug and alcohol prevention programs into school health curricula, first at the middle school level, then in high school and elementary schools.

International Conference of Young People in Alcoholics Anonymous (ICYPAA)

PO Box 22987
Denver, CO 80222
e-mail: advisory@icypaa.org • website: www.icypaa.org

The ICYPAA was founded for the purpose of providing a setting for an annual celebration of sobriety among young people in Alcoholics Anonymous. The number of young people suffering from alcoholism who turn to AA for help is growing, so ICYPAA helps to carry AA's message of recovery to alcoholics of all ages.

Join Together

580 Harrison Ave., 3rd Floor
Boston, MA 02118
phone: (617) 437-1500 • fax: (617) 437-9394
e-mail: editor@jointogether.org • website: www.jointogether.org

Formed in 1991, Join Together works to support community-based efforts to advance effective alcohol and drug policy, prevention, and treatment with specific programs for youth. This organization leads initiatives to help communities respond to the damage caused by alcohol and drug abuse among adults and youth.

National Center on Addiction and Substance Abuse at Columbia University (CASA)

633 Third Ave., 19th Floor
New York, NY 10017-6706
phone: (212) 841-5200
website: www.casacolumbia.org

Former US secretary of health, education, and welfare Joseph A. Califano Jr. founded CASA in 1992. This nonprofit organization conducts surveys and provides information about youth drug and alcohol use and prevention methods.

National Institute on Alcohol Abuse and Alcoholism

5635 Fishers Ln., MSC 9304
Bethesda, MD 20892-9304
phone: (301) 443-3860
e-mail: niaaaweb-r@exchange.nih.gov • website: www.niaaa.nih.gov

This federal agency's purpose is to conduct and support research in a wide range of scientific areas regarding alcohol consumption, prevention, and treatment. It provides information about alcoholism, ways to prevent and treat it, and statistics, including ones specific to youth.

The Partnership at Drugfree.org

405 Lexington Ave., Suite 1601
New York, NY 10174
phone: (212) 922-1560 • fax: (212) 922-1570
website: www.drugfree.org

Originally named the Partnership for a Drug-Free America, this nonprofit organization engages parents, scientists, and communications professionals to help families raise drug-free children. The partnership provides parents with information and training tools that they can use to help prevent their children from using drugs and alcohol.

Substance Abuse and Mental Health Services Administration (SAMHSA)

PO Box 2345
Rockville, MD 20847-2345
phone: (877) 726-4727) • fax: (240) 221-4292
e-mail: shin@samhsa.hhs.gov • website: www.samhsa.gov

This federal agency works to help people who are in need of recovery from or at risk for mental or substance use disorders. SAMHSA publishes up-to-date information about drug addiction and treatment with specifics about youth drug and alcohol use. It also provides grants for research on substance abuse among adults and youth.

For Further Research

Books

Lisa Bakewell, *Alcohol Information for Teens: Health Tips About Alcohol and Alcoholism.* Holmes, PA: Omnigraphics, 2009.

Sean Connolly, *Alcohol.* Ontario, Canada: Saunders Group, 2011.

Justin Gass, *Alcohol.* New York: Chelsea House, 2010.

Jarold Imes, *Never Too Much—the Remix.* Winston-Salem, NC: Abednego's Free, 2008.

Nicholas Lessa and Sara Gilbert, *Living with Alcoholism and Drug Addiction.* New York: Checkmark, 2009.

Tamara Roleff, *Issues That Concern You: Alcoholism.* Farmington Hills, MI: Greenhaven Press, 2010.

Jennifer Storm, *Blackout Girl: Growing Up and Drying Out in America.* Center City, MN: Hazelden, 2008.

Periodicals

Jane Anderson, "Youth Drinking Yields Emergencies," *Pediatric News*, September 2010.

John Cloud, "Battling Addiction: Are 12 Steps Too Many?," *Time*, January 27, 2010.

John Cloud, "This Ain't No Wine Cooler," *Time*, July 17, 2008.

Rochelle Craig, "Teenage Addicts Are Not Born Bad, They Have a Disease," *Daily Mail* (London), October 5, 2010.

Neil Johnson, "Alcohol, Drugs Slow Teen Development," *Janesville* (WI) *Gazette*, March 17, 2010.

Leicester Mercury (UK), "The Problem for Youngsters Is Boredom," September 22, 2010.

Larry Printz, "New Study Finds Parents Have Big Impact on Teen Safety," *Norfolk Virginian-Pilot*, October 4, 2008.

Sue Shellenbarger, "College Parties Minus the Beer Binges," *Wall Street Journal*, February 16, 2011.

Nancy Stevens, "Getting to the Bottom of Underage Drinking," *Norfolk Virginian-Pilot*, February 6, 2011.

Maia Szalavitz, "Does Teen Drug Rehab Cure Addiction or Create It?," *Time*, July 16, 2010.

Claudia Wallis, "What Makes Teens Tick," *Time*, September 26, 2008.

Wall Street Journal, "In Search of Alcoholism Genes," February 8, 2011.

Internet Sources

Centers for Disease Control and Prevention, "Underage Drinking," July 20, 2010. www.cdc.gov/alcohol/fact-sheets/underage-drinking.htm.

Bill Hendrick, "Family Dinners Reduce Teen Drug Use," WebMd, September 22, 2010. www.webmd.com/parenting/news/20100922/family-dinners-reduce-teen-drug-use.

New York Times, "Teen Drinking Diaries," June 25, 2010. http://roomfordebate.blogs.nytimes.com/2010/06/25/teenage-drinking-diaries.

SADD, "Statistics," January 2010. www.sadd.org/stats.htm.

Michelle Trudeau, "Teen Drinking May Cause Irreversible Brain Damage," NPR, January 25, 2010. www.npr.org/templates/story/story.php?storyId=122765890.

Source Notes

Overview

1. Quoted in Alcoholics Anonymous, "Young People and A.A.," 2007. www.aa.org.
2. Quoted in Alcoholics Anonymous, "Young People and A.A.," 2007. www.aa.org.
3. Anonymous, "I Drank Because of Him," ReachOut, 2009. http://us.reachout.com.
4. Quoted in Michelle Trudeau, "Teen Drinking May Cause Irreversible Brain Damage," NPR, January 25, 2010. www.npr.org.
5. Quoted in Nancy Shute, "5 Ways Parents Can Prevent Teenage Drinking," *U.S. News & World Report*, Health, April 15, 2010. http://health.usnews.com.
6. Newport Academy, "Teen Alcohol Detox Intervention," 2010. www.newport-academy.com.
7. Everything Addiction, "National Underage Drinking Prevention Campaign Focuses on Parents of Young Teens," May 18, 2010. www.everythingaddiction.com.

How Serious Is Teenage Alcoholism?

8. Quoted in Wright State University Boonshoft School of Medicine, "CAM Testimonials: Kevin's Story," December 17, 2007. www.med.wright.edu.
9. Bill Urell, "Alcohol Withdrawal—Is It Dangerous?," Addiction Recovery Basics, 2010. http://addictionrecoverybasics.com.
10. Quoted in Wright State University Boonshoft School of Medicine, "CAM Testimonials: Cathy's Story," December 17, 2007. www.med.wright.edu.
11. Roxie Norman, "Testimonies: Growing Up with an Alcoholic Parent," Helium, 2011. www.helium.com.
12. Sarah T., "I Sold Many Things to Get Cocaine," About.com, September 5, 2007. http://alcoholism.about.com.

What Are the Dangers of Teenage Alcoholism?

13. Quoted in Bethany Vaccaro, "I Drove Drunk and Killed Two Sisters," *Glamour*, February 2011, p. 129.
14. Quoted in CBS News, "Study: Teens See Binge Drinking as No Big Deal," April 6, 2011. www.cbsnews.com.
15. Quoted in Amanda Gardner, "One Therapy Session in ER Can Cut Teen Violence," MentalHelp.net, August 3, 2010. www.mentalhelp.net.
16. Quoted in Kristi Jourdan, "Police Combat Binge Drinking," *Las Vegas Review Journal*, April 12, 2010. www.lvrj.com.
17. Quoted in Alcoholics Anonymous, "Young People and A.A.," 2007. www.aa.org.

How Is Teenage Alcoholism Treated?

18. Shawn H. Treatment Solutions of South Florida, "Testimonials," November 2010. www.mytreatmentsolutions.com.
19. Ironwood Animal Therapy Blog, "A Horse Is a Horse Is a . . . Therapist?," June 30, 2010. www.ironwoodmaine.com.
20. Michelle Bolyn, "Adolescent Group Therapy Benefits," January 26, 2010. www.livestrong.com.
21. Quoted in Maia Szalavitz, "Does Teen Drug Rehab Cure Addiction or

Create It?," *Time*, July 6, 2010. www.time.com.

22. Quoted in Kristen Daum, "OKC Sober School Reforms Drug-Addicted Teens," *NewsOK*, July 27, 2008. www.newsok.com.

Can Teenage Alcoholism Be Prevented?

23. Quoted in Partnership at Drugfree.org and Metlife Foundation, *2009 Parents and Teens Attitude Tracking Study Report*, March 2, 2010, p. 22.
24. Quoted in Family Day, "About Family Day," 2011. http://casafamilyday.org.
25. After-School All-Stars, "Factoids," 2011. www.afterschoolallstars.org.
26. Quoted in *Science Daily*, "Greater Religiosity During Adolescence May Protect Against Developing Problem Alcohol Use," June 22, 2010. www.sciencedaily.com.
27. National Crime Prevention Council, "Promoting Drug-Free Social Events for Youth," 2011. www.ncpc.org.

List of Illustrations

Index

About the Author

Leanne K. Currie-McGhee lives in Norfolk, Virginia, with her husband, Keith, and two beautiful daughters, Hope and Grace. She has been writing educational books since 2003.